Praise for *The Ballad of Cherrystoke*

Melanie McGee Bianchi writes with graciousness for the reader: it feels like she's invited you on her porch to tell you these stories because you need to hear them. She also shows graciousness for her characters, allowing them the full spectrum of humanity no matter what space they occupy in the world.

Steven Dunn, author of *Potted Meat*

Yuri in "Abdiel's Revenge" says: 'If there's a main idea in all those ballads, in all of Appalachia, to my mind, it comes down to this: bones in the river.' *The Ballad of Cherrystoke* is a collection about Appalachian people (not characters, not stereotypes) with secrets and trust issues, brain injuries, prison records, sh**ty jobs, broken hearts, urges and needs and fears – but Bianchi is observant and wise, kind but unflinching, an archaeologist; she listens, and excavates, and through rich and luxuriously meandering prose pulls those bones up onto the bank for us to touch, and taste, and feel. This is the best debut collection I've read in years. Melanie McGee Bianchi is sharp, and tender, and brilliant.

Meagan Lucas, author of the award-winning novel *Songbirds and Stray Dogs* and Editor-in-Chief of *Reckon Review*

The narrators in this c⌐   ⌐s to
observe and report their   ⌐ as
striking and surprising   ⌐ew
and unique voice to Apɼ

D1334099

Hea   ircle

Brilliantly weaving together original narratives with elements of the real Appalachian mountains and their people, these stories reveal startling details that create immediate, visceral impressions of complex, haunting characters: their secrets, their fears, and their anguish... Like the mountains they inhabit, these characters are a mercurial parade of stunning beauty and terrible pain.

Elizabeth Baird Hardy, author of *Milton, Spenser, and the Chronicles of Narnia: Literary Sources for the C.S. Lewis Novels*

The complex, the quirky, and the sublime are interwoven with humor, love, and above all, grace, in contributing to a tradition of powerful storytelling. The landscape is steeped in the voices of the people.

Tony Robles, author of *Cool Don't Live Here No More – A Letter to San Francisco* and *Fingerprints of a Hunger Strike*

Bianchi has created worlds that seem simultaneously magical and rooted in the grit of rural reality – a vexing combination that dares the reader at every turn. Her rich characters grow within us in uncomfortable and compelling ways that force the next page turn.

-Annette Saunooke Clapsaddle, author of *Even As We Breathe*

The characters in Melanie McGee Bianchi's debut collection, *The Ballad of Cherrystoke* – gritty, determined, shrewd – are modern balladeers, narrating remarkable stories set in the Appalachian South. Beautifully unusual, told in penetrating, straightforward prose, these stories reveal genuine, universal truths, affecting and unforgettable.

Susan Beckham Zurenda, award-winning author of *Bells for Eli*

Through deep lyricism and a sharp eye for detail, Melanie McGee Bianchi's stories peel back the quotidian moments of everyday life to demonstrate the complexity of what it means to live in a world crafted by both our desires and our choices – and what it means when those two elements don't always coincide. *The Ballad of Cherrystoke* is a powerful collection that uncovers the music of humanity that emerges each time a person interacts with another person in a complicated and changing world. It's an extraordinary and haunting debut.

Adam Clay, director, Center for Writers at the University of Southern Mississippi; author of *To Make Room for the Sea*, *Stranger*, and *A Hotel Lobby at the Edge of the World*; editor of *Mississippi Review*, co-editor of *Typo Magazine*, and contributing editor for *Kenyon Review*

The Ballad of Cherrystoke

and
other
stories

MELANIE MCGEE BIANCHI

A Blackwater Press book

First published in Great Britain and the United States of America by
Blackwater Press, LLC

Copyright © Melanie McGee Bianchi, 2022

Printed and bound in Great Britain by Clays Ltd, Elcograf S.p.A.

Library of Congress Control Number: 2022933245

ISBN 978-1-7357747-4-9 (paperback)

Cover design by Eilidh Muldoon

Interior illustrations by Giuseppe Monterisi

This book is a work of fiction. Names, characters, organizations,
locations and events portrayed are either the product of the author's
imagination or are used fictitiously.

Blackwater Press
120 Capitol Street
Charleston, WV 25301
United States

www.blackwaterpress.com

Contents

Introduction

It was like reverse writer's block. The flood came first.

Writing this book felt urgent. I worked on the manuscript infrequently, at odd times, during intense hours stolen from an extremely hectic life, for about four years. Whenever I got the chance to add to the growing collection, the words reared up and boiled over like they had an attitude problem. Getting it down was easy.

Except it wasn't. Once the work was finished, I got anxious. I changed my mind and decided that the project had been almost impossible.

Who were all these people? What, exactly, had just happened?

Because the motivations of my characters came to me fully formed. Their voices were hurled whole from the void – even the quiet ones. Making their journeys real the whole way through became an obsession, no question.

Some stuff was decided. Yuri in "Abdiel's Revenge" loves Pammy because he hates rules. Siobhan in "The Ballad of Cherrystoke" loves Shad, her favorite blanket, and her possum visitor in equal measure, because that's how her post-accident brain works. I have a main character whose job it is to name others. I have two main characters whose names are never revealed at all, so defined are they by those closest to them.

Me, I don't have deep roots anywhere, but I've lived the biggest portion of my life in the Southern Appalachian Mountains, so that's where I've set most of the plots. If gentrification, the changing cultural landscape, brings trouble in some of these stories, it's simply because the book's action is set in the last twenty-odd years, and that stuff has happened here – is happening.

Living where I do, and having a musician husband who plays many instruments, and also having a bit of a morbid imagination, I've long been fascinated by the murder ballads common to the Appalachian range. These are a subset of the fiddle tunes that can be traced some 400 years back to their origins in the old country: the bulk of early settlers in Southern Appalachia were Scots-Irish.

My interest is hardly unique. People, even young people, still play these haunting tunes. Painters paint whole series inspired by them; writers write novels and plays about them. The old songs get "discovered" all the time. When it comes to ballad study, I can't claim one shred of the knowledge or the dedication of the historian or the purist or the busker on the street corner.

But dread and melody and regret aren't confined to one era. So, if a murder ballad – ancient or invented – pops up here and there, in this book, it's only because I thought it fit the story. The story right now.

The Ballad of Cherrystoke

They sent my twin brother to the Cherrystoke School of Professional Crafts to learn how to make fancy acoustic instruments for a living, but he only lasted one week in that prison before he ran away, hitchhiked back into real life, and ended up at the lake resort where I worked, hoping to stow out with me in employee housing.

Slowly, I informed him I had a schedule now and didn't have time to be hiding runaways. But I'd missed him – I knew I had missed him when I saw him in my doorway, shimmering a bit, undefeated. I followed him around, kicking at the heels of his disgusting Chuck Taylors. Then I made him a pallet on my floor, a row of dank cushions covered by his own sleeping bag. I wedged it under a window with a million-year-old box air conditioner where he was sure to get a sore throat sleeping every night.

He liked history. He talked about Lake Revel being a manmade reservoir. It spread its seventy-mile shoreline over the North Carolina line – one of those pretty craters the Tennessee Valley Authority once poured all their efforts into. It happened back during the Depression, he said.

The fact of a drowned-out town lurking two hundred feet under that diamond water hadn't stopped anyone from vacationing at Lake Revel for the rest of the century; their affection for it was just encouraged and encouraged. I knew there was at least one dead church at the bottom of Revel, and on good days, off-duty days when my short-term memory came winking back at me, I would start to shiver during my afternoon swim, wondering suddenly what it might feel like, going all the way down and getting the bottom of your foot poked by a steeple. I hoped I would remember to tell my neurologist, who viewed any abstract thought as positive. The doctor wanted to see my imagination grow back on its own, uninfluenced by my confusion.

Shad was lucky to find me! Not everyone who worked at Lake Revel Lodge had their own room in the employee bunkhouse – you had to be an old-timer, having worked every season past the brink of sanity, or else you had to be like me; that is, viewed by management as having special needs.

The bunkhouse was an ugly building on short stilts, low and gray, with a line of rooms on each side. You either faced the parking lot, a bad scene with no hope, or else you had a view of the lake, not as good a view as the Lodge guests got, but a reasonable flash in between pine trees and the musky buttonwoods, plus a tiny deck; you could go out there after your shift and catch the breeze. The lakefront rooms seemed like the better fate at first, except as summer wore on, they got soft and sad, rotting inward from all the mildew.

My brother was always talking about hopping trains, serious trains, freight trains – he had that addiction for bringing back the hobo life in all its miserable freedom. The bunkhouse was a freight car; at least it did its part to look like one. It looked like a freight car parked for good and going forever nowhere. Shad liked that. He could hear me getting better, bit by bit. "That sounded like the old you," he said. "Combined with the new."

I told him that his being there would definitely get me fired, and that he couldn't make any noise of any kind, including and especially playing his great love, this old banjo he had, an SS Stewart older than the lake. So I sat on my single bed in my murky lakeside room, on top of this tea-and-cream-patterned blanket, *matelassé*, my mother called it, borrowed from my childhood bedroom – really my best possession – trying to write out some rules for him on the back of an envelope.

But I couldn't keep my damaged brain on that task for long, and he was tactful enough to not mention it. And then everyone who mattered got hooked on the sound of his banjo, anyway. Shad played the clawhammer style, the desperate old minor-key ballads; since he was a fugitive, he made a point of being patient with anyone who called it bluegrass in ignorance. Somehow, he got management to give him an easy part-time job in outdoor maintenance, stuff like repairing the Lodge's wooden deck chairs and cleaning Kit-Kat wrappers and used condoms out of the reeds, and it wasn't long before he and I were in this together.

He was sophisticated, my brother. He mentioned the condoms with haughty distaste, which reminded me I had to change my behavior, now that I had a real roommate. Some of the college-boy waiters from the city, Kirk and Elliott and this jolly, giant, rosy-cheeked guy who seemed to be covered in Ds – his real name was Damon Doherty and his friends called him Deez Nuts or D-Dawg, nicknames I never understood – they still knocked on my door after the dinner shift, toting Bacardi and weed like a Disney prince would hold roses.

I wanted the sex; ever since I recovered from my accident, I felt that lush ache inside me almost every minute. Why would anyone want to go around any other way?

But something about it all was different now. The way the guys set their gaze upon me – you know that harsh smile men get, once their goodwill drains out? Their lowest eyes? Anyway, now that Shad was here, my brother here in my room, it was my greater pleasure to turn the others away.

"If you become a real freighthopper, you have to get a railroad-track tattoo to prove you're legit. You have to get it on your *face*." That was Lacey, who worked with me in housekeeping. She'd been demoted from her server's position at the Lodge restaurant because she refused to shave her armpits for the benefit of diners' appetites. The sight of it had ruined morning waffles for an important lady from Atlanta. She saw the evidence when Lacey bent over her one morning in her work-issue green polo shirt, during the breakfast rush, setting down orange juice for the lady's towheaded grandchildren.

Everyone was pushing Lacey to make a stink about the discrimination, or at least to quit. It was midseason, so the attrition rate – that was Shad's phrase – was already pretty bad. But Lacey seemed jazzed about the fame. "I was only their morning drudge, anyway," she said. "I never got dinner shifts. No one could handle my personality."

The incident had loosened her self-regard. Here she was now, floating unasked with my brother and me, flirting and chirping in a raggedy string bikini, her updo sparkling with barrettes.

She was competing with the water. She absolutely was.

Shad said he was going to pack up Little Miss – that's what he called the banjo; he was quite ridiculous – and head west soon, and he just might have another tattoo, indeed, by the time any of us saw him again. Likely more than one.

He could sit cross-legged with a loose bag of American Spirit tobacco in his lap, poised like a golden egg between those knobby knees, and roll cigarettes without moving anything else around him. He was the little scrappy type and a terrific swimmer, even in the dark; he had knifed his way around the east bend of Revel, past the golf-club entrance and the tiny public beach and wrestled this old inflatable boat out of the bracken, a discarded commercial raft that would have been more at home on a river.

Shirtless but wearing ratty swim trunks, he seemed to be planted in the middle of the raft, keeping the balance like a forest gnome.

Lacey sat up on the prow like a figurehead. He let her.

The sun on the water would make you go drowsy and half blind, if you had a mind to submit. I curled myself into my portion of the boat, sitting crosswise to the others with my legs hung over the edge, my arms wrapped around my waist. I didn't wear bathing suits; I felt best in my cut-off jean shorts and purple T-shirt from Dixie's Dairy Bar down the road. The best place! Not a place but a *palace* – I thought of it as an ice-cream palace. Chocolate and peanut butter in one flavor. Mint-chocolate-chip. Raspberry cheesecake.

I couldn't taste well anymore, except for what was very sweet – something to do with my brain injury. The mixed-together ice-cream flavors were my favorite; I liked to try to sort out every lick.

I was calm, breathing slow, and when I opened my eyes, I saw a water snake bobbing toward us, coming between the twigs and tree litter in the silver lake wavelets. In my head I told the others about it, but by the very next second, I had forgotten to mention it – that was the core of my trouble.

I'd gotten hit by a car, from the back, during my daily run, ten miles from home. The morning sun was in the driver's eyes and I was running in the middle of the road, like any champion – it was pure misfortune.

They had to tell me what happened. I still had to take their word for it, because I remembered nothing. After a while, four weeks or so along in the rehab center, I did start to recall the beginning of my senior year, months before the accident. I suddenly saw myself, as though in a movie, storming queenlike into a morning AP class in a new pair of platform flip-flops, my mind greatly loaded with drama.

After the car hit me, I had actually sailed through the air, witnesses said – I had tried to fly! Where I landed, headfirst on a country highway, was on my prefrontal cortex. It was the same place they gave people lobotomies. Someone told me this. Who? I didn't know, but I figured out what they meant: I would be dumb forever. Which meant placid to the point of vanishing.

It wasn't true, though. I was mostly placid, but I was mad a lot, too. The fury came in gusts so brief I don't think I ever spent it twice on the same idea.

I got mad about the quivering divot in my throat where the tracheal tube had been inserted, during my short coma. I saw it in my dingy bathroom mirror one morning, getting ready for a day of scrubbing pubic hairs down the drains of the Lodge's new garden tubs.

It was like it was my first time seeing it, although the accident was so long ago now – two years and more. I whapped the mirror with the back of my hand, to make it disappear. I said "fuck you" a couple times to my reflection.

But by afternoon, I had forgotten the hole. Really, they said, I had so much to be thankful for. The ability to walk. Life itself. They'd had to trepan my skull when my brain swelled, and after the surgery, starting in rehab, my hair had grown back a new shade, a different brown and wilder all over, and I liked it, especially now that it was long again. I often took wonderful care of it.

Maybe I was calm, but I wasn't dumb – I knew the attention I got now wasn't the same as what had been mine before. The anti-seizure medicine made my eyes dilated and spooky. Yes, I could walk, but I swayed to the right, and my voice, once it finally returned, was run down with slush. I couldn't make it sound like the thoughts in my head.

The first year of my new life, in my new slowed-down body, I grew gradually thicker, and now, in year two, I was thicker still. Sometimes I thought my flesh expanded while I slept. My bra started to make sore tracks against my ribcage, and my underwear got so tight I felt that it took my breath away. So I stopped wearing underclothes altogether; I sunk them in the lake and never thought about them. Some days I felt freer than I could ever express. I should have called Mom to take me to the mall for new stuff, but every time I went to pick up the phone, I forgot exactly what I needed.

Until Shad came, I didn't do much. I was glad to be on my own again, glad to have a job. I wondered if I would drive again some day, but besides that, I didn't want much. I ate with the other employees, in the Lodge's back kitchen, and I would get a ride to town sometimes for ice cream and snacks and to buy magazines and paperback novels. Back in my room, I would try valiantly to read them – but the endless lines of type were only arrogance; all the same and no meaning in them that would stick.

It could be ninety degrees, but I was mostly cold. I laid under my coverlet and watched VHS tapes on my crappy TV. Nature documentaries, or Disney movies with songs that soothed and tortured by turns. I would never run after cross-country trophies again – I would never again dominate my peers. But I was here, and here was here.

The lake pulled down Appalachia in one rush – this lamenting purple-green sunset – before night folded in. It didn't even have to be a full moon. Once it was properly dark, my brother and I sat on our little deck and listened to the foxes sweetly threatening their own mates across the water, these harsh kitty cries. Later on, it was screech owls, and hard to tell the difference.

He rolled my cigarettes for me and lit them, keeping the flame low before handing them over. "That girl wouldn't last two seconds on a train – scared shitless of a water snake," he said in his shallow hectic accent, a twang I falsely regarded as his alone. In my head I floated, sorting out the pool of his words. The way he said it, "futile" sounded like *few tile*. Like it should.

"Lacey," I said, "is just a rich college girl." I didn't know if she was or not, but I knew Shad hated rich college kids, and there sure were enough of them at Lake Revel Lodge, working the short season before they went back to their college lives. It seemed safe to assume.

He tightened his lips around his cigarette for a moment and sucked to make it glow hard. It was the same thing as his nod. His black T-shirt, it was so faded it looked like it was erasing itself.

I was awful to him, I called him a "No Count" because it was a funny, old-fashioned term, and he himself had taught it to me, taught me to use it against him. He was gold. I don't think he was ever awful to me.

He blew out his smoke in a show of rings. "You should have been a college girl yourself by now, right, Shivvy?"

Shivvy was short for Siobhan, which no one here knew how to pronounce because they didn't have straggle-haired New Age parents obsessed with Celtic folklore, like we did. Shad showed the influence more. He had the knowledge of the old music, how it came from Ireland and Scotland to infest itself in the Southern mountains. He wore a Celtic cross necklace, this winking hunk of pewter.

Our parents wanted him to make money with a job that was dignified and artistic; that's why they sent him to Cherrystoke to become a luthier. I thought it was nice of them – I didn't have Shad's capacity for resentment – I didn't resent anything – I didn't know how anymore.

When I was a baby, my mother could not keep clothes on me. All these Polaroids she showed me after the accident, squeezing into my netted hospital bed with me, trying to lure back the parts of my memory she thought were relevant – I was naked in every one, or at least shirtless, wearing bottoms puffed up like bloomers, defiant, holding someone's wildflower I had yanked up by the roots. In one photo, I was maybe two, standing in a canoe in this same place, this very lake, with only a diaper on and not even a life jacket to save me if I fell in.

"But I like it here," I said, remembering that my brother had spoken. "If I stay through closing I get this same room in the spring. Mom said I could come back."

Shad ran his rough little hand over his bald head. My poor twin brother, he was only twenty years old and already his hair had fallen out. You could feel the tragedy of it inside him; surely someone had done it to him – I would never imagine he was to blame. "Genetic," he sometimes said, refusing to talk about it otherwise.

I don't think it hurt him as much as he might fear. He still had fierce cheekbones and these chilly important eyes. I had to remind myself to try and keep Lacey from liking him, and a couple of the other college girls, too, and even harsh old Dinah, the head of housekeeping, who used words like "cove" and "holler" and "y'uns" like no one was waiting around to dispute her. Dinah said she'd grown up with the old ballads; she said she was the real deal, and she wanted to sing along with Shad's Little Miss after dark, smoking with us, her voice menacing and filled with grime:

> Well, they had not been at sea two weeks
> I'm sure it were not three,
> When she began to weep – She wept most bitterly.
> "Ah, why do you weep, my fair young maid
> Do you weep for your golden store?
> Or do you weep for your house carpenter
> Who you'll never see no more?"

Shad would let anybody who knew the words well enough sing along with the banjo; he kept playing and he kept his mouth closed. Now, alone with me, he curved his hand – they called the gesture a claw; I told him time and again it looked more like a paw – and started his strokes, down, down, the *chuk chuk chuk* rising in between the notes like mist. He finally muttered the answer in his own voice. He sang:

> *I do not weep for my house carpenter.*
> *I do not weep for my store.*
> *I am weeping for my tender little babe,*
> *who I'll never see no more.*

I was cuddled against him, the twin *matelassé* coverlet stretched tight to fit around us. I wanted more and more in my lungs tonight and asked him to roll me another American Spirit, and some of whatever else he had.

We were drinking hard. I cried a little, when I thought to do it. Shad talked about spending the winter in Mexico and bringing me back a bleached-out animal skull from the desert, if I wanted one.

This made me gasp. I told him I wanted to feel the top of his little bald head – I had never done it yet! He laughed, but only at my eagerness, and said I could.

I made a point to pause, needing to do it right. I pulled my whole soul into gentleness. I took my left hand out of the blanket, the hand that worked best. I pulled it out like a brave snake and touched him. I turned my fingertips into tiny bugs, trailing back and forth over that skin-covered skull, careful not to leave behind an impression. How could anything be so hard and soft at the same time?

"I guess you shave it now," I said when I was done, tucking my hand back in my blanket. "You look better that way, no hair at all."

"I agree with you," he said. "But it's not recent. I started shaving my head when you were in the hospital, Shivvy. Remember? That time when you were bald like me."

I did remember, when he reminded me of it. I asked him to tell me the story of our family.

I called Shad my twin brother, although to be honest, we weren't related by blood. But if you were able to ignore the past and just line up the facts as they were, the surface miracles, it all worked. Both of our birthdays were in January. He was five-feet-eight-and-a-half inches tall, and so was I. Weirdly, this made him seem short, although I was considered tall – I had been the second-tallest girl on the cross-country team.

Our names started with the same sound, *Shhh*. We were both allergic to penicillin.

My mother met Shad's father at a New Year's Eve contra dance in the Piedmont when we were both sixteen, about to be seventeen. Before this, we had grown up as only children, but it was clear that this *brother*, as I was being forced to consider him, had suffered way more from that particular condition. He just didn't seem to have a will of his own. I could see he was only trying to be like his dad, even listening to the same old music.

He was a copy, and I was a star. I pulled down all As with almost no effort at all, and I would get an athletic scholarship, too – it hadn't happened yet, but my coaches were optimistic. I had picked out my colleges, my favorite and a couple of backups.

I wore my makeup thick and hot to contrast with my plain little mother, who never did anything to improve herself. I was proud of my sharp tongue; it had brought me friends in swarms.

"Let us behold this curious spectacle: I call them Thing One and Thing Two," I'd whispered one night to Mom, who was from the north and had a big education, though you wouldn't know it from her life choices.

I draped one arm around her little poky shoulders. I swept the other arm theatrically at the sight: these two sudden, unlikely males in our own ceramic-tiled kitchen, making salad and vegetarian lentil stew for dinner. They were as alien as a mouse you find in your cupboard.

Mom *tsked* at me. She left me and went over to her new husband. Their love had been instant and absurd; they got married at the courthouse and she wore a flowered dress that brushed the floor. He handed her a knife, blade end pointed away from her. They chopped tomatoes together for the salad. Raising me, she had been practical. Now she was off in heaven.

No, not a mouse at all – it was a possum, just a little baby. It crept in our sliding glass door one night, abandoned by its mother or lured by our crumbs, and curled itself up in Shad's bedding. He said he had dreamt all night about an Irish banshee struggling around him, trying to get herself free, her wings caught in the sleeping bag.

When the idea of a wild animal finally occurred to him, he unzipped the bag quietly and there it was, silver-furred and quite spiteful, clinging with its naked pink feet to the red-and-black flannel. It opened its mouth and hissed at us.

"I didn't know they did that," he said, stroking the possum's foot. I was afraid he would begin collecting whole litters of stray possums, because his backpack – this bulky thing that rose higher than his head, when he had it on – it was filling up. He'd hitched a ride into town with Lacey and had stolen some items from the Army/Navy store, a few things necessary for survival on the trains, which were not, he told me, always the friendliest places. We were still at Lake Revel Lodge, but I wasn't sure he had a job anymore.

"I wonder where the mama is," I said, laying spread-eagle on my bed in my green polo shirt and khaki pants. I was already dressed for work; I wore a watch and I had two alarm clocks to make sure I got to my morning shift on time. Management had recognized me as the only employee who had made it so far through the season without once being late.

It had come August, the month when a great storm split the lake every afternoon, leaving behind not a chill, exactly, but the promise of news from another direction. The out-of-town college kids were working their final week. The crew shrank but got rougher, older waitstaff coming in with experience from hell – fey, desperate men with sad stories and swollen noses, and women who looked and talked just like Dinah, because they had known her forever. *I've got girlfriends who could work circles around these young clowns*, she said. *And they're ready to start any time.*

"Play for me, No Count," I said to my brother. "I have exactly ten minutes left to be in this room."

"What'll you have, Shiv?" he said, drawing himself up cross legged, picking up Little Miss but facing the possum a bit, too, like he was singing to both of us. "'Omie Wise?' 'Pretty Polly?'"

"No," I said, slowly. "No murder ballads. No dead girls."

He hummed and strummed, pondering, before continuing a song of his own he'd been working on. His voice had gone raspy, sleeping under the air conditioner so long.

> *I don't want to go to Cherrystoke.*
> *I'd rather be here, and I'd rather be broke.*
> *I'll ride the rails and I'll be free.*
> *I'll find some old gal to ride with me.*

He sang in his lightest register, because of the wild animal in the room. I listened with my eyes closed. "'Old Gal' sounds stupid," I told him, and he nodded, setting Little Miss aside and reaching for his bag of tobacco.

My memory, it only went back a few years without help, and my brother, he had never not taken me seriously in those few years, which I really considered my whole life. Before my accident, I had barely known him, but I had known him well enough – that is, I had never known him to be rebellious, or to have so many dark notions about freedom. *You changed when I changed*, I think I once realized, but the idea never made it to my mouth.

"I'll get some old rodent to ride with me," Shad sang *a cappella*, to me and to the possum. I giggled myself into hiccups, half asleep. He kept a straight face.

That night, after dinner and a game of horseshoes I watched at the lakeshore, I came back to an empty room. The space under the air conditioner was empty. No pallet or sleeping bag there, no dirt-colored banjo. I didn't see the possum anymore, either.

It had been a long time since I got to be alone in my room, so I took off my damp work clothes, accidentally stuffed them in the bathroom trashcan instead of the hamper, and wrapped my body in a luxurious fluffy towel my mother had sent to Lake Revel with me. I sat on the deck in my towel-robe to feel the air off the water. Any second, that sultry breath could decide to change.

At first, I was furious, finding Shad gone like that. But since he had only gone up to Dixie's Dairy Bar to bring me back a mixed hot fudge and caramel sundae, it would be ridiculous to complain. All I had to do was wait for him.

The knock on the door made me jump, it was so rough and formal. "Come in, I guess," I called. "But don't come out on the deck, I'm not dressed." I was still trying to see into the coming dark, wondering if the baby possum would be back. What turned me around was the sense that my visitor wasn't bent on that question.

"Hey, Girlie Girl. Long time no see."

My eyes adjusted, and my mind followed. I saw Damon Doherty D-Dawg Deez Nuts. There he was, out on the deck with me, as jolly and rosy as ever – so many healthy teeth inside him, so much shaggy hair, grown down to his shoulders like an outrageous fib.

"Girlie Girl" had been a joke between us, before Shad arrived. The joke was how this big, grown boy couldn't pronounce "Siobhan." He couldn't find the time to do it right.

But he had been my friend, once. "I know you're … off," he had told me kindly, the first time we talked. He'd actually winked at me, once he said it – where had he ever learned something so glamorous? "It's pretty obvious you're off," he repeated. "Or at least it's half obvious half of the time." He laughed. "It's not so bad, though." He had taken my hand with great ceremony – I think we were the last ones at dinner that night. "I'm an open-minded guy. I actually think you're pretty. You're pretty sexy, Girlie Girl, if I'm going to be honest." Hearing that, I touched my own hair.

"I always speak my mind," he had said. "That's just D-Dawg talking."

He hadn't asked me if I was lonely. I wasn't – I was happier than most people here, that was certain. But he was – he was lonely, he said, and thought I must be feeling it, too. His girlfriend had cheated on him, before he came here. So he was left lonely and sad. I told him I had had a boyfriend in high school, before my accident. Sometimes I could picture him very well.

Now, on my deck, Damon spread his arms out wide, in apology or triumph. "It's my last day," he said. "School starts next week."

I stared. There just wasn't anything else to look at. When he leaned in and his rum fumes reached me, I sniffed like an animal, because I had lost my manners a long time ago.

"What are you doing out here with no clothes on, Girlie?" he said, watching the top of the towel that I had tucked underneath my breasts. It was too late for me to remember the towel was supposed to go over them.

"Oh. Wait, though. Shad will be back in a minute," I said. "He's at Dixie's getting me ice cream. He's at –"

"He's not at Dixie's," said Damon. He liked me, but he never liked me enough to keep from interrupting everything I tried to say. "He's down in Lacey's room, got all his hobo shit with him. I just saw him."

"I think you must be wrong," I said. "He must be going to get me some ice –"

"Bet he's going to take her with him, freighthopping," said Damon. "And you'd better get used to that particular situation."

I was bent over my *matelassé* coverlet, thinking of lost ice cream with what felt like a very old sorrow, while Damon grunted away somewhere far above me, my long hair wrapped up in his fist as his personal handle. The sound of his loud body falling frantic against my naked behind made me think of the motorboats that would pass our piece of shore on Lake Revel, grinding the water so far out of place the waves would slap the bank for five minutes afterward.

I could hear a familiar sound start up in my own throat, the sound that marveled at such a turn of events. My thoughts were alive – that or my confusion.

I felt my mind had made a mistake, some time earlier in the evening – a mistake I couldn't remember anymore. It could have been a year, or even a hundred, that passed while that lonely man was in back of me and on top of me, not inclined to free himself – a rabid baby possum riding its mother.

So I was thrilled, after a spell of centuries, to see Shad finally come in the front door. I wanted to tell him about these grand new pictures my mind was making: Damon who was just like a motorboat, spoiling the lake. Damon as the absolute worst possum around. My brother would approve of it all.

My brother! That odd, nodding, bald little spitfire. "It's Shad," I said. "It's No Count." He looked like the good round sun coming up early, that's what he absolutely was, moving toward me in such an unneeded rush.

Since Shad was here, I could take my own time to talk. But he didn't have Little Miss with him; that was the bad thing. I didn't recognize what he was carrying – I didn't even recognize the way he was moving. I could tell you, with no one allowed to correct me, that my twin brother was not singing.

Abdiel's Revenge

My lover, full name Pamela Jean Galloway, she clung to whims and omens to get her through a full day. She'd see some little shadow as a threat, another sort of shadow as a revelation. If I ever had a problem with her, it was only that. I'd been on this earth half as long as her, but goddamn it, I knew a genuine crisis.

The most important event of Pammy's life, Abdiel's Revenge, hadn't even happened to Pammy herself – it had happened to one of her ancestors. There was a ballad about it already and some slick outsider, a professor or close to it, was wanting to write a play.

Pammy was proud as hell of the story; she didn't seem to care who stole it or used it. In truth, she had lived her whole life around it. And here she was now, fifty!

She was actually fifty years old, you know, and freer than anything, skittish her whole life about being married, although her grown-up daughter took a different view of that institution – lived down the road, hitched to some redneck I didn't mind too much. They had given Pammy a couple of grandkids, twin boys: matching baby hellraisers, is all you need to know.

All that, and Pammy still seemed like a child herself. You could call her a cougar, since I was still in my twenties, but she had no taste for blood. Already I knew way more than her, at least about practical things. It was me pointing out to her that her favorite jeans would last longer if she turned them inside out before washing them. It was me making the better omelet.

Pammy Galloway! *Fuck.* She was this flirty little *matryoshka*, so tiny she could still shop the Juniors department, so immature she bragged about it. She swept her frizzy hair up so it would spill right back down. Her skin glowed from being in the garden. Attracting the pollinators, she said. I helped her stake sunflowers and build a little raised bed for the cherry tomatoes. It went on like that; we had a good time.

You're thinking that because I'm a convicted felon, some fifty-year-old piece of ass is the best I could get. Or that I needed a mommy more than a lover – because that's the way of some men, free or no. Approximately ninety percent of the time, the toughest guys are the neediest, and if you need examples of that, I'm the one to provide them.

But I got sick of explaining that shit really quick, because with Pammy and me, it just wasn't the case. She wasn't my substitute mom. My mother was never like Pammy, not even remotely.

My mother knew her duty, so don't misunderstand me. Cold but solid. You know that type? Nothing like the young moms you see around here. Some of these girls – hell, I went to high school with most of them – these girls would sell their own baby for a ten-second high. My mother wasn't like that. She had her plans for me.

You have to know I am the youngest of four, and my brothers and sister, they lead respectable lives. One brother got a scholarship and went to a big university, found a job making real money; the other was put in charge of a menswear shop at the mall, married with a few kids already. I was the error. The ferocious surprise. My parents worked hard, like most immigrants do, but they got worn out by me.

Pammy Galloway, though – she was warm all over. She was old, for sure, but she didn't hardly see it. Horny as a teenager and up for anything. Have you known that kind of woman? The night we met we were both at Ravenel's, this bar at the river.

My post-release curfew was finally lifted. I was free to roam all night but I was staying with my sister, sleeping on the couch in the living room of her apartment. My sister was a first-grade teacher, always decent to me. I was far from content, though.

So Pammy was at the bar, throwing eyes at some guy, but I said a couple slick things and soon she was drinking with me instead. She informed me I had an accent, as though that wouldn't occur to me. "Just an itty bit of one," she said.

I'm strong, but I'm not so tall, so I was charmed to observe that her head only reached my chest. I called her "Munchkin" and "Shorty" before I landed her real name. We got far away from the craft-beer geeks and were opting for liquor drinks, sunk down in a couch by the fire pit, next to the back deck strung up with Christmas lights in all seasons.

Some singer-songwriter was sitting on the deck, strumming this damn fine acoustic guitar, this gorgeous thing probably worth two thousand dollars. He faltered over some minor chords, singing so sad. Something about a giant mall where his grandma's house used to be. After each song, Pammy paused our conversation to clap. You could hear the river behind us, North Fork, with its back-talk rhythm that does not quit.

Those little claps, they already had me smitten. I was raised hard with the old-world manners, you know, and I liked her politeness. Otherwise he was only playing for tips, rich-boy guitar notwithstanding.

She was wearing a lace blouse and denim everywhere else. Hair pinned up high, earrings swinging down low. So it was frustrating, too, because I'm a wolf. I cannot lie about that – I am a wolf for real. And I had been hungry a long time. Spring was turning to summer and I was jumpy as hell, nowhere to rest my energy, no real routine anymore to keep me straight.

I was still missing the slog of prison life, that predictability with no responsibility: dawn count, garbage food. Nap. Work. Weights. Repeat. Not that I would have ever confessed it.

I was hungry to fuck, hungry to get on with life, whatever my real life was fated to be. And there she was, torturing me, clapping for this other guy, then turning to me, attending me with those same hands. She cupped her ear so she could hear me better, and when she did that, her charm bracelet jangled. All that cheap, happy silver! That was her; that was Pammy

24

Galloway. The bracelet had two hearts hanging off it, each one etched with a "J," the first letter of both grandsons' names.

She put the other hand on my knee, and she stroked it; our age gap, it gave her no worry. And who am I to blame her? I was looking good. My shoulders were as wide as any mountain, right then; my arms were dead rock.

It's true that my first month inside, I lost an incisor, got snagged one day by a high chin check – the dark hole in my smile was the ugly souvenir. I won the fight, though. I'd gotten hard, locked up, way tighter in body, in mind – hours on end to lift and to read. Hours to brood, go into something like prayer. My grown-out hair was glossed back in a ponytail, and I had on my own silver chain, a good one, the one my sister had kept safe for me. It held a charm, too, an icon of Boris and Gleb, martyred sons of Prince Vladimir – dearer to me than my real-life brothers, those self-involved *mudaks*.

Besides my one sweet sister, all my other family, not to mention my two or three so-called friends, and even my ex, who had stopped e-mailing me after the first two weeks, once she found out the county jail charged for that privilege – they all said the same thing. They hugged me tight, then got shy. They said I looked a lot older since getting out, that I'd definitely aged more than eighteen months in those eighteen months.

They said it like I was supposed to laugh right along. I couldn't believe how unchanged they were, how worthless: bloated faces and shallow minds. I was expected to smile? Agree with them and slap my felonious knee? Well, that would not be happening. So I commenced cutting them off, one by one.

I went home with Pammy that first night. The lust we had, it was dead equal, both sides – you don't need me to tell you that's rare. I went home with her, you know, and she asked me to stay. I did stay. I stayed, and the weeks bled into months.

So there we were, this one morning, and her droopy eyes, they were begging my wisdom. In this damp cove where she lived, something was always happening that was more or less stupid. Today we were dealing with this insane bird situation, some pea-brained fucker that had mistaken our closed bedroom window for his path to freedom. It blasted us awake, hitting the glass.

The meat of him, it swooped down with a thunk, and then he'd fall away, beaten. A blank minute of suspense, and goddamn if he didn't do it again the exact same way. Over and over.

– Flutter, flutter, floof. Bam.

At first I just banged my pillow at the window to drown out the sound. It wasn't a bluebird, for Christ's sake, or even a robin. It was nothing. A thick gray bird slamming your window one time, that shakes you, but it's no big deal. You just want it to know better, right? But this shithead – he was persistent.

"It's trying to get at us, Yuri," murmured Pammy, closing her eyes again and crawling onto my chest. "It means something."

"Jesus God!" I said. "Stop looking for omens. There are bigger problems afoot, *Tsyganka*." I called her Gypsy because of all that silver she wore, day and night. Then I added a long stream of Russian swear words, because it was no effort for me and Pammy found it arousing.

I wasn't born here, in this muggy blue-green confusion. I remembered my home country, a couple of dreamlike flashes – a tower of wind; a deep, happy shouting I couldn't pin to one man. I grew up knowing my native language first, and by the time I was a young man, a man of the American South but not really, never a hundred percent or even seventy-five, I could slip in and out of any situation I liked.

The other Eastern Europeans here, a lot of them were eyeball-deep in the local Slavic Pentecostal church like sheep in the rain. Once I got out, I sometimes snuck into one of those yellow-grain pews myself, just to hang my head. Something did hurt somewhere, in me, but I sat alone.

Pammy, though, she'd talk about her own hurts all day. She explained how her arthritic complaint wasn't due to her age; it was, in her own words, "pure-T hereditary." She had had it for years, her old dead daddy had had it, this cousin and that cousin were likewise afflicted. And speaking of family, all these joint issues, they were part of the same family, too, so she said: rheumatoid arthritis, psoriatic arthritis, *ankylosing spondylosis.* I raised my eyebrows at that last one, doubting there was any other Galloway alive who could pronounce such beautiful nonsense.

I never could observe anything wrong with Pammy's joints, nothing off about her joints or any other part of her body, that's for sure. But I would never call her a liar. If you believe that shady disability checks plus a singlewide sunk forever on family land adds up to lucky, then Pammy was lucky. Sure, she had some problems in her head – about as many as me – but her view left to right was Caney Knob, Bell's Mountain, Turtleback Ridge, on and on. It was the same view those outdoorsy freaks down in town were paying for all kinds of ways, staying in thousand-dollar-a-week cabins in between camping and kayaking and driving the Blue Ridge Parkway way too slow, on the prowl for meaning.

Pammy was a bit of a freak, too. She trafficked in amethysts and astrology and a tarot pack, the whole New Age disaster, but in her I didn't mind it so much. My girl had her own style going; somehow, she pulled it off.

She wasn't a hippie or a homesteader, playing house in the mountains. Like me, she was practical when she had to be. If she had ever told me to call poison ivy "Sister Ivy," a charm to keep it from biting me, that would have been our last chapter.

Her family went eight generations deep in this hole, and the old ones still called it a holler. The mountain was named after them; likewise the fucked-up road, half dirt, pure treachery – Galloway Ridge Road – and I would never make that up. I was superstitious myself, it was bred into me, and if Pammy claimed to be a natural witch, I wouldn't go against her.

By the time my own family landed in this muzzle of hills for a home, I was five years old and Pammy was somewhere close by, I guess, being a single mother. So now here we were, my folks twenty years settled and more, but the locals couldn't even spell our last name yet, much less give us our own motherfucking mountain.

She did throw away her Ouiji board for me. What a beauty she was! So the rest of that occult garbage? I let her keep it, because this woman, she satisfied me every day.

– Flutter, flutter, floof. Bam.

That bird did not quit. We got up for real so we could suck down some coffee – I made it better, it had turned into my job – me shirtless and grouchy but handsome, no lie, my morning boner defeated inside my boxers, though, and Pammy tapping her feet on the cold floor and clutching her empty mug, waiting, cute and hyper in my T-shirt plus pastel cotton drawers. There was a silver ring on every one of her fingers – an ankh, a Celtic cross, a lovers' knot, etcetera – but she never wore panties with lace, nothing extra on her clothes to suit my fancy taste.

"Does it have rabies?" Pammy said. I had to remind her that only happened to mammals.

– Flutter, flutter, floof. Bam.

"Goddamn you to hell!" I shouted at the bird. The worst part was, I jumped every time, practically whacking my head on Pammy's low ceiling.

"You raising your voice makes it worse," she informed me. She drawled on about her love for birds, but I knew better: she didn't love them too much. "This can't go on, Yuri." Then she used the word "portent," licking around it like a haughty kitten. Like "portent" was a diamond inside of her mouth. Like it was my job to find it.

She wanted me to kill the bird, I could tell she did. That was the drama in her, like a real disease. To tell you the truth, I hadn't killed any birds since before I began liking girls. But Pammy assumed since I'd gone bow hunting as a kid, in these woods, where it wasn't the clear cold firs of my homeland but instead hardwoods and hells of dark-green laurel, the forest smelling all summer like something ripe to be bred – she figured I could bust out the backwoods skills anytime I liked.

I loved how she made a point of my name. *This can't go on, Yuri.* I loved her anyway, if it comes down to that.

The real horror on the mountain that week came before this brain-damaged bird. It came from one of our neighbors. Four college students were stuffed in this little rental cabin next to Pammy's property, some dummy's one-time vacation home long gone to rot. I always thought the house's exaggerated A-frame looked like a pair of hands tilted together in prayer. "Send me a mudslide, Dear Lord, and take me home," I would say to Pammy, riding shotgun in her beat-down truck. She was always dropping me off and picking me up so I could hustle some clean cash from handyman gigs, and I felt the least I could do in return, besides eat that sweet pussy, was make her laugh a little.

So one of these kids, the tall mushroom-faced one who was flunking out of the little state college down in town – it was obvious he was home too much, watching porn or playing video games or something all goddamn day – he'd been arrested for exposing himself to women late at night, a few miles down from campus in this industrial area. The scandal went online soon enough; I brought it up on my phone and Pammy hung her little chin over my shoulder so we could read it together, our mouths hung open.

The college kid, the perp, our neighbor for months: his name was Phineas Karter Westmoreland, and we had never troubled to meet him. His kink was parking his white Subaru under an isolated overpass, wearing this trench coat, but of course nothing underneath. According to reports, plenty of people had seen him before, sitting for hours in his car, just like that.

"Idiot fuck," I said, scrolling. Phineas Karter Westmoreland was lucky to have a car. Lucky to even be in college.

Then, once he got up his nerve, always well past midnight, he'd walk around a few desolate streets, drinking a Red Bull because he wasn't twenty-one yet, approaching any female around – "Hey, can I ask you something?" – and spreading his coat apart like curtains, a grand stage for his silly cock.

His victims, I was hoping they laughed. Laughed once they were safe. Because his whole method: I mean, what the fuck? So old-fashioned it was funny. Too old-fashioned for belief.

"Seriously?" I said to my screen. "A trench coat? Must be a history major." Pammy landed a punch to my right trapezius, but I'd kept up my lifting, you can count on that. There wasn't one muscle on my torso that could be moved.

The flasher was caught as fast as you'd expect, but as a man, as the man of the house with a girlfriend to protect, I couldn't let this stupidity rest. I thought maybe the rest of those *idiotas* next door were of the same mind as their buddy and needed a Yuri-style talking to. But the perp's housemates had voiced their horror about the flashing, you know, prim as nuns now, every one of them. They told the cops how they all barely knew the guy: he had just answered their ad for a fourth party, and furthermore, they'd been about ready to kick him out. He hadn't paid his part of the rent yet.

This pussy's parents had posted bail, and I guess Phineas Karter Westmoreland was back home with them, wherever that pretty place was. His old teachers queued up to the press to say he had been a promising student, yes, but always a bit of a loner.

And now the air over there had gone dead. No partying, you know, no music. It was like that pervert's crimes had happened right there in the house, not twenty miles of switchbacks away down the mountain. The fact of it lingered like dirty smoke.

His white Subaru wasn't there anymore, but the other guys' cars were. They weren't brand new, none of them – not the cars I would buy if I procured the means. But they were new enough: late models with Thule racks on top and oval bumper stickers from breweries. The cars didn't tear up and down the road anymore, flirting with the ridgeline; they went quietly, as though they carried serious scholars.

My body still as a corpse, I watched the A-frame from Pammy's kitchen window, where I was doing her dishes. I saw the flash of a TV in there, sometimes the shift of a grimy blind.

I'd gone to sleep wondering how to handle the situation, then got ripped awake by that ugly bird. So now I had a winged animal abusing me, just another guard doing his count, and my nervous lady to calm down, too. It just never stopped.

But wait. I never told you yet about Abdiel's Revenge. So, you know how mountain people hang on to shit way too long? It had that aspect to it, but it was still a good story, like most of the old ones are.

Back in the winter of 1880 or '81, Pammy's great-great grandmother, Christian name Abdiel, right out of the Old Testament – but called Abi – she went psychotic from being cooped up in a tiny cabin way too long. Only one or two windows. Hell, maybe none. She had two babies clinging to her, a toddler and a newborn, and an unfaithful husband, Leland Erskine, who was always drunk off his ass, you know, enjoying that homemade stuff. According to the tale, Leland was a bearded redhead, a brute, probably taller than Abi's daddy and brothers combined.

She was seventeen years old, for Christ's sake. Night-black hair and not even full grown on her wedding day, from the look of the creepy old photo they always ran with her story. But Abdiel Pegeen Galloway Erskine, already she had a limit, and she wasn't taking her man's shit one more day.

She loved the rascal in him, though, so her wrath went astray. She got stuck, is what I think. Maybe she was dreaming the whole time. What she did, one cold night, after Leland was passed out and those babies tucked in asleep, she snuck over to the cabin of her husband's widowed mother, went down a path with a lit branch of shagbark hickory in one hand and a big jar of shine in the other. But she didn't plan on drinking. Instead, she soaked the old lady down, right there in the bed, and torched her. She lit the rest of that woman's cabin on fire, too, just to make a good job of it.

Killing her mother-in-law hadn't been in the girl's blood, before then. She wasn't born bad, which might have been easier: at least I think so. After she completed her evil deed, poor Abi threw herself in the icy North Fork, and that was that was that.

The ghost of the act, though – that didn't die. Due to Abdiel's Revenge, there were Erskines and Galloways who still wouldn't communicate. This was supposed to be important, but the family squabbled so much anyway, fighting their own, how would you ever know?

They were kind of trashy, if I'm going to be honest. You could call me an old-world snob and I wouldn't resist you.

Still, though. Passionate arson and suicide by drowning, no whining or forethought, just do it, ha ha – to me, that is pretty badass. If there's a main idea in all those ballads, in all of Appalachia, to my mind, it comes down to this: bones in the river. And that's cool.

I'm not one of those nostalgia freaks who gets all choked up on the local culture, but I understood it. Because my people, they had stories, too. A thousand pounds of winter, a thousand pounds of blind rage. Maybe Abi got turned around and torched the wrong villain – though if it wasn't the mother's fault her son turned out bad, I don't know whose it could be.

"Usually the man's the killer," Pammy would say to me, up on her high horse. Like all her family, she had to repeat a thing to infinity to make sure you were feeling it. "Granny Abi reverses the ballad archetype." If she said it once, she said it ten times a day, like my sister practicing her piano scales once upon a time. Improving herself in the face of my agony.

That old story, it got Pammy so riled I got jealous, had to ask her who she was getting those big words from. I'm an asshole, I know it, always have been, to tell the truth – but I swear to the Lord she drove me to do it.

I'm not one to brag about what I was in for, but I don't grovel about it, either. It was B&E, and that's public record. "Aggravated" comes from dealing, going up the chain, waving my weapon around like I was hot shit. You could say it was my ego that took me down, and I would shake your hand. I'm not a gangster and I never pretended to be, but I hated authority like a snake hates the mouse it's choking itself on. I finally got hit after skipping parole meetings from some dumbass little prior, and I did my time, and now I could just be me: a man who was more than a mistake, growing younger day by day.

What Pammy and me had in common, we thrived on the deeper motive. Kill the mother and you kill the sins of the son. Make sure whoever's in your life wants good for you, only good, and turn to motherfucking ice the second you sense the opposite.

That's how we did it, you know. That was the only way. We glanced back, groped ahead, got our pleasure. You would do the same in our place.

She only wanted me to be happy, and that's what I wanted for her, too. There she was now; she had gotten tired of waiting for my superior-made coffee and she was down on her knees, that saint, taking me into her mouth like she was born for exactly that.

She loved me back, but right now she was buttering me up to do something about the bird. I moaned anyway, deep in her spell – not one among us is given universal strength – and I stroked her long hair with the gentleness of a prince.

– Flutter, flutter, floof. Bam.

"He wants in on this action, right?" In all events, I was a witty fucker, but this was dangerous: if I made her giggle, she'd fall out of her rhythm. "Pamela Jean Galloway," I whispered, an absurd hitch in my voice, tracing my thumb around the fairy curve of her ear. I would want a nap after her good work, but how a nap would happen under the current ambush I honestly could not say.

At that moment, the bird was saving me. Because before it crashed into my life, I might have been feeling a tug backwards. The devil pulling on my tail. I'd clocked the roommates' schedules by now; that was the easy part. Hell, I could pull weeds off Pammy's plants for an hour and not make it look like a vigil. I was a lot of things, a whole lot of things, but incapable – that wasn't one of them.

When the time was right, maybe I would ease my way into that empty A-frame, just to scope. I needed to dredge up more evidence on that slimy little pervert, find out why he had wanted so badly to be caught.

I wasn't in it to help the cops, mind you: just to spruce up my game for when I met Dumbfuck Phineas face to face. I knew who tended to get locked up and who was apt to go free, and right now he was out there somewhere, breathing the same air as me.

– *Flutter, flutter, floof. Bam.*

Or maybe the bird did have rabies. I'd never seen or heard a bird act like this. Pammy called the bird "it," but I felt he was male.

If he did have rabies, his bird brain wouldn't be right. He'd be off, you know, he'd be confused, and before I did anything else on this brand-new day, I could finish him with my bare hands. With one hand, probably – squeeze him right out of life till his body burst with relief.

Like my own.

It's Called Overwintering

Their state was known for the best views and the shittiest teachers'
salaries. Things got so tight that year they were requiring all the
teachers' aides to double as bus drivers, no saying no, but so far
CG had said no, softly, and survived. She was mousy or she was
slippery, according to who was doing the criticizing. This freedom
wouldn't last forever.

Today they had one of the older, uglier buses, plus a bus
driver no one recognized, borrowed from another school in their
system. CG knelt on one of the middle seats over the wheel,
facing the aisle, pivoting her head like a sleepy owl to keep track
of the excited fourth graders on either side of her.

Mrs. Morrison, the teacher, sat right behind the bus driver,
standing once in a while, looking them over. She was from
Florida and she'd been teaching elementary for twenty years,
but she was new to North Carolina that year, with the expected

energy of a transplant. By the second semester, her class was well on track in English Language Arts, in math, in science, in everything. She was progressive – she had them sit on yoga balls, to increase their concentration. But assessment tests were coming, so she couldn't relax her vigilance, not yet – she was letting her shrill spots show.

She whimpered lushly about the weather. It was still cold, in April, in the mountains. It wasn't anywhere near bonafide spring. But she wore a sundress anyway, under a light cardigan. Like the seasons would just roll toward her in any direction she wanted. She fumbled for the top button now, closing it around her cleavage with her long fingernails, painted salmon pink.

Mrs. Morrison was distractible and often unpredictable, but she couldn't scare anybody. She didn't even know her phone's GPS wouldn't work on the Blue Ridge Parkway, and now she'd gotten the whole bus off course, trying to get her class to their field-trip destination. They were taking two loads of fourth graders to the Turbyfill Experimental Forest so the guides there could demonstrate the scooping of tadpoles into a mesh net, and rage lightly at the children about their role in protecting the planet. By this time, the other bus with the rest of the fourth grade in it was out of their sightline. CG assumed they were already at Turbyfill, right on time.

School buses weren't even allowed on the Parkway. There weren't any guardrails up this high; that was part of the experience. Maybe you would get appalled by that view, skid sideways into one of the scenic overlooks, and keep going right over the edge – in fact, somebody's motorcycle did this about

once a year, as though the vehicle itself, much less than its rider, had just that in mind.

CG knew the dangers. Of course she did. She'd grown up here. Even though she was half Mrs. Morrison's age – could be perceived, out of context, as the teacher's own sullen tomboy daughter – she could have told her a lot. But she was just a teacher's aide, and they didn't pay her enough to give away all she knew. She paused in her own vigilance and snuck a look behind her. There was the gray thrust of Ramsey Mountain ahead, still winter-bare. That meant the Ramsey Mountain Tunnel was close.

She reached up subtly and cracked the metal window. The April wind stirred the wisps of her short hair under its wool toboggan. Her face was droll and stubborn; her chin was shaped like an old Ugg boot. A knockoff. CG hadn't drunk enough coffee that morning. She tried to whisper without moving her lips: *I'm just here for the ride.*

Mrs. Morrison's real kids were in college somewhere, grown up, out of state. She and her husband were Empty Nesters now, Mrs. Morrison said. She talked about her husband with a solid, condescending affection. That man wasn't going anywhere. There was so much Mrs. Morrison was safe from, really, except her other children, these twenty fitful souls she was paid to mind.

She meant well; she really did. Maybe the teacher's voice was her only problem. Her tone, it leaned toward affected. When CG's mind was only coasting, sometimes Mrs. Morrison's "please" came to her ear like "police."

CG lived with a few roommates in a sagging apartment, the bottom right quarter of a boxy old house in the slowly gentrifying historic district. They were all resourceful – they made a formal dining room and a covered porch act as extra bedrooms. Their apartment was full of mold. It might be just mildew, or it might be the kind of mold known to kill. Maybe the house would be torn down instead of sold and renovated, like so many other, similar houses, and then they could go after someone for all the toxins in their bodies. A class-action suit. When they weren't squabbling with one another, some of them kept logs of their little illnesses, just in case.

Meanwhile, the end of each month turned into the first of the next one, over and over, and they split the bills, CG and her roommates, sometimes even down to cents. But that didn't mean she was making it.

The hip bistros and microbreweries paid better, but they wouldn't have her. She lacked energy, went the impression, though she secretly wanted to be a singer. Her full name was Cass Ginger Harrington, and her mother was an older mother who had had her at the age of forty-three, courtesy of a younger man, a disappearing mandolin player. So the story was told.

Now Mom was a hippie senior citizen who wouldn't or maybe couldn't retire, drove in fifty miles one way every weekday from her cabin way up in the hills, this little thing she and her gaggle of Boomer friends had built – CG thought of it as a shed – to teach folkloric studies at the smaller, more expensive of the two colleges in town. It was the woodsy private one full of well-spoken, protesting types.

It was all nice people there, aware and intelligent – nice people mincing into nice futures. CG couldn't get in; her high school grades had been borderline awful. Also, she didn't want it. She wanted bloodletting, an explosion to turn heads – but she didn't know how to get that, and she was too caught up in crushes and weekend drinking, which wasn't the same trail at all.

CG's second-to-last lover, Natalya, who was older, thirty-two, was up north now, long gone in Maine, working as a law-enforcement ranger at Baxter State Park. It was a place so remote that people who wanted to die but had no access to weapons, or else no stomach for them, went there to get lost on purpose – to starve to death alone, with no witnesses.

That would literally take forever, CG said, wrapped in Natalya's arms. The concept was astounding. It was despicable and almost funny.

She didn't want Natalya to go. Natalya was so healthy. Her thick, long braids smelled like the bulk bin at the co-op, and there was no way to tell how she stuffed her big goddess ass so neatly inside those government-issued uniform pants every day.

Natalya was successful. Her attention made CG feel alive, protected, like she wasn't a directionless girl with a hangover but only an amusing little minx with a lot of learning left to do. *That wouldn't be an easy way to kill yourself*, said CG, almost panting for more information. *It wouldn't be painless. You'd go insane first.* She tried to remember if she had ever Googled how long it took to starve to death.

But it still happens, and that's one thing we're trained to watch out for, said Natalya, who was prudish about details. *People going into the park without any kind of outdoor gear. It's the main warning sign.* She hadn't shed a tear.

So then CG tried to tell her that Maine would be too cold and isolated. But Natalya said loneliness was part of the appeal. The Blue Ridge, the Smokies – they were too settled for her, too full of tourists; that's why she was leaving. The Southern Appalachians felt claustrophobic to her. *I need more space to breathe,* she said. *You say people go insane from isolation, but I'm the opposite. Too MANY people around is what threatens MY sanity.*

So CG had to give in. *You're bound to go away,* she told Natalya, defeated enough to steal a phrase from her mother's music.

The lover after that was a busboy at the old Olive Garden near the mall, where CG worked as a hostess on weekends. This time she got to be the older one. CG was twenty-three and the busboy, Daniel, was only twenty, but broad-shouldered like a bonafide man and charmingly full of anger and foolish phrases, some that sounded like Spanish and others that might have been gang code or only stolen, misinterpreted treasures. Daniel said his father ran the streets in Miami. *Living the life.* But that his mother was just a piece of white trash fucked up on pills. *Unfortunately,* he added, when CG winced.

He told her he was preparing every day for his own future. He told her he planned to retire within the decade, and he only answered her folksy guffaw with a raised eyebrow. Daniel was suave.

So where did you get all this alleged money? CG asked, to get to know him better, after their first time together on the squashed, odorous futon in the basement of his older brother's house, where he stayed. It was apparent soon enough that Daniel, who said he enjoyed porn but that he didn't let it rule his life, could only get it up for doggy style. During sex he had cupped his palm over her mouth, in a distracted way, when she moaned loud enough for someone to hear. But even with all the drama, he had only lasted a minute – not even long enough for her forearms to get shaky from supporting both of their weights.

Where do I get my money? he repeated. His drawl came and went, a mockery that probed feelingly around different locales. *Supply and demand, Hermosa. I start my real work when all the rest of y'all go home for the night.*

She predicted she would soon sour on his self-importance. Maybe she wasn't slick enough to sell drugs, like Daniel. Maybe she wasn't dedicated enough to a single path to become an authority in a uniform, like Natalya. But she was enough herself to know that if you went to peel them out of their costumes, Daniel and Natalya were pretty much the same person doing the same damn thing. The poise was a sham; they were waiting around but to judge.

Just last month, at the elementary school, some interesting graffiti had appeared on the wall in one of the girls' bathrooms, above a toilet. THIS IS HORSESHIT, it said in cartoon bubble letters. And how could it be otherwise? It was the best joke, uniting all the teachers for a while, the newer ones and the ones who'd worked there through their prime – kept trudging back, semester after semester, past the point of absurdity. (*Too MANY people around is what threatens MY sanity.*) For a few minutes, the idealists and the old skeptics were all laughing together.

The message shifted, depending on where the reader put the emphasis. THIS IS HORSESHIT. The little perp! Had she meant it literally, acknowledging someone's huge, unflushable shame? Or was she just as weary of the school-year drudgery as everyone else – the aggressive hurdles of the calendar, units harder or duller than they should be, the grubby winter weeks when it was cold enough to snow and liberate all of them for a day or two, but the snow wouldn't come?

It was CG's job, then, to escort the girls in the class to the bathroom, whenever one of them had to go, and stand outside the stall door with an air of supreme neutrality, arms crossed, while the student finished her business. All the aides on the hall had to do the same for their own classes; this policy would stand, it was declared, until the vandal confessed.

Eventually someone's mother who found out about the ordeal pointed out that it was unfair – that a boy could just as easily have snuck into the girls' bathroom and written the offensive statement. When that seemed farfetched, she added that you couldn't condemn every child for the actions of one. (*But it's a girl's handwriting*, CG said at some point, to somebody. Bubble letters were a thing that did not change.) A meeting was arranged by PTO members, and it was someone's enlightened idea that the aides should be invited, so CG got to go. *What lesson are we trying to convey, anyway, with such a punitive approach?* asked one dad. He wore a Surly Bobcat Pale Ale T-shirt and had a beard that moved like a furry hype man when he talked.

Finally they decided to have the children visit the toilet in pairs. By this they were assuming that the vandal had acted alone, and would never fall to making art with an audience around. After a couple more weeks the routine went back to normal. Everyone had different ideas about who had done it, but by then a new problem came up and THIS IS HORSESHIT was forgotten.

Mrs. Morrison discovered that four of her classroom's students who sat together in a square of desks – Finn, Jaxon, Sierra, and Ainsley – were playing a strange game. It was imaginative, she said, but she felt it was inappropriate. Or had the potential to be. She'd seen a lot, over the years, but she hadn't seen this.

They called themselves The Family.

Finn was the father. He had black-framed glasses, like a miniature indie-film critic, and purple and blue and green streaks in his blond hair, and he went by Big Daddy. It was all his idea, but everyone had a role. They could snap out of it when they had to, enough to stave off a reprimand, but left alone they played their parts with great consistency. They didn't even break from it during recess. *This little scenario of theirs*, Mrs. Morrison called it. She said it to CG one afternoon, after dismissal, when CG was down on her knees, scrubbing hardening papier-mâché out of the grubby old carpet with a Brillo pad.

They had sculpted and painted solar systems for their space unit – blaring, lopsided balls that were drying over the windowsill in a happy row. The planets pulsed in their neon colors. *I made papier-mâché planets back when I was in school*, said Mrs. Morrison. *So did I*, said CG. *It's honestly a great memory*, she added. It was.

Anyway, Mrs. Morrison said, assuming a forceful yoga posture at her desk. *I'm on the fence about this little scenario of theirs. Finn is the root of it. It makes sense for him to take on an alpha role, but I don't want it to become a distraction.* She was distracted herself, frowning through a line of e-mails, one of them probably from Jaxon's mother, who banned all toy weapons at home and didn't like that a rubber MineCraft sword had recently been used in a school play.

Jaxon was Little Brother, the son in The Family. CG was surprised he had agreed to the role, because Jaxon was already small for his age and felt the stress of it. He snapped rubber bands in unwise directions and kicked chair legs. But he'd been more mellow lately, since joining The Family, and no one could truthfully deny it. Tall, bossy Ainsley was Mama Bear. Sierra, an effortless achiever but quiet about it, was Older Sister.

They were supposed to be paired off on the bus in a system of Mrs. Morrison's that separated all the troublemakers, but she had turned to argue with the bus driver about their route, because things were serious now and they were getting further and further away from Turbyfill Experimental Forest. The members of The Family, who weren't exactly troublemakers but might be headed that way, softly found their way to one another. CG had been sitting alone, but now Ainsley was suddenly on the seat next to her.

Ainsley reached across the aisle to grab Jaxon and pull him on her lap, which was strictly forbidden. Everyone knew they had to keep their hands to themselves; this was instilled almost every hour. Finn was in the seat in front of CG, and he convinced his bus buddy to swap with Sierra, so now Big Daddy and Older Sister were together.

Come on now, said CG. *Y'all are going to need to switch your seats back as soon as she figures out you moved.* Her voice had no real duty in it. She wanted to see them transform into their roles. It was way more interesting than a play.

The evil bus driver has gotten us lost. Mama Bear is protecting Little Brother, said Ainsley, hugging Jaxon close. Ainsley was wearing a fleecy, rose-colored North Face jacket. Jaxon laid his head against her chest and nodded with an exaggerated look of terror. He moved to suck his thumb, and CG cracked up. You couldn't not.

What do you say to that, Big Daddy? she asked, turning to Finn. She knew if she started in with it herself she was close to stepping off some cliff. Maybe she'd been on the edge of doing that ever since the day started, anyway.

Finn was already assessing the situation through his black glasses. CG remembered the days when the smartest kid in the class never would have been the most popular. Things were different now. She heard adults, adults older than her who didn't work with kids or even have their own at home, complain about *young people* having too much screen time, not enough play time – that's the first thing they always said, once they learned she worked with schoolchildren; they seethed and seethed about it – but they didn't take into account what was better about kids today. That the smart ones were cool, now. That all the kids seemed sharper. They zeroed in on the bullies together: she had seen it. And pretty soon there weren't any bullies, or anyway no mean kids in the way CG remembered. No one scorned anyone's brand of jeans or speech impediment or unusual sandwich filling – not that she ever caught.

Maybe that was really the issue adults had with the Kids of Today, she had theorized. They were becoming so good at bully sniffing that even the grown-up bullies had to rewire their wrongdoing. CG's mother liked to say that cowardice was a form of tyranny, but it was hard to tell if she was talking about her vanished love, the mandolin player – who was merely a ghost story, as far as CG knew – or about some human-interest thing she'd heard on NPR, or about her buff-colored rooster, Scruggs, who liked to attack from behind when the mood took him, burying his spur into a human ankle before backing off and letting Pretty Polly or Ola Belle, his favorite hens, snooze under him the rest of the morning.

Big Daddy's got you, said Finn. *We can hike back on the Mountains to Sea Trail. We just can't turn east, because the sea would be about three-hundred-and-fifty miles away and I don't want you kids to drop dead.*

Finn might have the highest test scores, but Sierra was known as the class reader. She put her thick book into her backpack and turned her attention to them. *We can camp*, she said to Jaxon. *We can make a fire out of sticks when we get cold. Don't worry, Little Brother. The bears will still be hibernating.*

But Big Daddy was still full of facts. *Bears don't truly hibernate this far south,* he said, shaking his rainbow hair around. *It's called overwintering.*

You should be asking ME what bears truly do for the winter, said Mama Bear, and got huffy when everyone giggled. But that's who she was.

You holding up all right, Jaxon? asked CG. Jaxon looked so content, so unlike his usual jittery self, cuddled up against the much bigger girl. *It's Little Brother,* he corrected her.

Oops! she said. *My bad.* Older Sister smiled at her, then shyly looked down at CG's arm that was resting on the seat back between the four children. She patted the sleeve of CG's sweatshirt in a courteous way – like CG was one of The Family now, but could still be the teacher's aide, too, if she needed to be.

A touch of wind that was colder than the breezes before it came through the cracked window, like a little decision.

She didn't need a new name to become part of The Family. They still called her "Miss CG," like they had since the start of the year, and she liked it. When she said it back in her head it sounded like Missy G. It was how she pictured herself when her dream stuttered from jazzy torch singing, full smolder in a floor-length black dress, to hip-hop.

She could always go back to sleeping in the attic loft at her mother's cabin, a space too tight to even stand up in, and keep working, save enough money to move somewhere else and meet some new people. Or she could get her courses back on track at the community college, try to do better, get in a real school eventually. Not her mother's college, but somewhere down the mountain, away from anyone's old ideas of her. Greenville or Charlotte. Maybe Atlanta.

The last time she was at the community college, a student she knew only by sight had OD'd from pills right in the back of the library, studying in a carrel. Some giant of a boy about eighteen or nineteen, sheepish but decent-seeming. The bigger shock was when one of her instructors, English Composition, quit over the tragedy. Tears in his eyes, he told the class he couldn't handle the scope of the youth opioid epidemic in this town. It was overwhelming him. He said it was wearing his soul down and making him question his career choice, plus everything else in his life, really. Some in the class had cried with him, while others, like CG, only shivered in acute embarrassment.

Up at the front, the air was turning to crisis. Their driver, the stranger, had eased the bus off the twisting snake-lick of Parkway and into the wedge of a scenic overlook. Then she got dramatic, heaving the gearshift into park.

But she was older than CG had first thought. She was an old woman. If she ever stood up, she would be no taller than one of the taller fourth graders, though strong and deeply smoke-wrinkled. She was about the same age as CG's mother, except Mom wore her gray hair long and braided down her back and this woman had hers cropped low, hidden from the world. A tuft of it was visible from the back opening of her baseball cap, taking the view behind her.

That driver, she sat unnervingly still for a moment until Mrs. Morrison leaned forward, gathering the courage to tap her shoulder with a salmon fingernail. But she wouldn't turn around. She just regarded them all in her long bus mirror. When she finally spoke, she had to unclamp her lips to let the words out.

I've got no mind to go further with these young ones till you figure out where this bus is meant to be. I know where it's not meant to be, and that's up on this Parkway.

Mrs. Morrison accelerated her fluttering. *Yes, of course. Of course. You can see that I am TRYING.* She didn't have a voice in her own repertoire to match the deadly announcement. She pulled her cardigan tighter around her shoulders. She stabbed at her phone desperately; she even shook it like a baby. She snapped her voice down the rows, meeting the younger voices that were rising now, the fourth graders scared or thrilled by the possibilities.

It wasn't that CG didn't realize what was expected of her. She knew exactly what she had to do. First, get the children quiet. Second, let Mrs. Morrison know that they had passed Turbyfill miles ago but that they merely had to find a way to turn around, take the detour down steep Highway 151 and do their best to cling to the curves and not lose their brakes, since that road was closed to trucks and other big machines – then hang a right at the old dam, and arrive at the experimental forest. Late but safe.

And third, least important but somehow necessary, once they were at their destination, CG had to find out whether the bus driver had known the right route all along, too. She was pretty sure she knew how to get the driver to talk. If they could get away from the others, they could share the pleasure of a cigarette.

She would keep formality out of it, no need for introductions. A few delicate topics would warm the driver up: where the trillium were blooming. What the spring time change did to exhaust the body. The exploding cost of survival.

Instead, she turned away from both the teacher and the bus driver, to determine where they were. She saw the brown forest-service sign: Ramsey Mountain Overlook. They had already passed through the tunnel, then, and she hadn't even noticed.

Look out the window, it's snowing up at the summit, she said to The Family. They crowded their heads close to hers. From their vantage point, almost five thousand feet up, you could see it coming over the hills, a wild white revenant confidently covering its ground.

Spring snows are the heaviest, said Big Daddy. *They come up from the Gulf,* he started to add, but CG shushed him gently. *Take it easy on all the info*, she told him. *You've got these others to look out for*, she said, indicating Mama Bear, Older Sister, and Little Brother with a magic wave of her fingers. *It's your job to protect them and keep them from getting scared.*

Mama Bear and Little Brother cuddled more tightly. Big Daddy nodded, and despite his authority, seemed to be waiting for further instructions from CG. Older Sister just watched the snow.

Good job, y'all, said CG. *Now you're coming together like a real family.*

She wondered how far she could go with all of it without being fired, right there, that day. Refusing to call these four kids by their real names, encouraging and deepening the charade –

that was bad. But the stage wasn't right for the drama. It would get a better reaction in the classroom, not here, where all was confusion anyway.

Grabbing them and marching them out of the bus would make a better story. And picturing it was a blast.

This is horseshit, she would tell them. *Let's go for a hike instead. The first one who finds a trillium gets ten bucks. But you can't pick it, because trilliums are endangered, and you'll get arrested. That's lesson one.*

She knew as much as Big Daddy, and maybe even as much as some of the paid guides at Turbyfill. *Nature never dies, even in the colder months*, she'd say. *Real life goes on when we're not all trapped in that vomit-smelling school.*

She wasn't worried about the snow because the ground had been warming up for weeks. It wouldn't last, and there wouldn't be any snow down in town, not a flake, but Mrs. Morrison, she couldn't take that on faith.

A Day on Saturn

I always said a man with a sense of humor was the only kind to be endured. When my husband Eugene was alive, he knew I went inside our pretty little outbuilding, sometimes, when I had to cry, and he was graceful about it. In his husky jester's voice, he referred to it as "Mother's Little Hidey Hole" – and for that, I tackled him around his knees and commenced tickling him where he could least take it. For a while we called it the gazebo, since he'd latticed it up the side for my climbing roses. They had a name, too: Joseph's Coat. Pedigreed.

But it wasn't really a gazebo. It was a proper place with four walls and electricity and a green metal roof – a far-enough jog from the house that Eugene had plumbed a toilet and sink in there, hidden behind a curtain I made up from some remnants in a ladybug print.

It started out as my husband's workshop. That man was going to get us rich in our coming old age; there was nothing truly selfish in his thinking. But Eugene didn't live long enough to make his woodworking projects turn a profit. He was talented, no question, just not born in the right time, quite. You should see what some people will pay for a handmade table, nowadays – give it out that the wood for it came from your granny's old tobacco barn, and before long you might need to sweep your driveway of all the cash raining down.

People used to call him a real mountain man, they did indeed, but he didn't grow out a beard for the look of it, the way they do now. Mostly he kept himself slick-faced; that was his kindness – I didn't care to get scratched, of a night, if I was going to be woken.

Eugene kept a real job, a family man's job, working for the highway department. He did his time, no question, and when he retired, he started planning to put in an apple orchard on our seven acres.

He decided we'd take some trips, too, buy us an RV, maybe, an older model, and visit some national parks – the great ones out west. He mumbled on about the Grand Canyon and Yosemite and Yellowstone. Eugene said Old Faithful erupted approximately every ninety minutes, and he would gladly wait that long and more to take my picture beside it.

One time, he rolled over in bed at three in the morning and rooted me up. He was agitated; his old-age insomnia kept him online for hours. *Let's drive up to Canada, gal,* he said, stroking my hip. *Get us some passports and get out*. He had a sudden notion to see the Calgary Stampede.

But not too long after that, my husband was gone. It was another morning, around seven o'clock, and I was in the kitchen, in my old flowered bathrobe and funny moosehead slippers, making our coffee. I was stirring, pouring the half-and-half, going over the drama of my fading night's dream – something about trying to make the cheerleading team, back at my old high school, and sobbing like a fool when they discovered my real age.

It was the same speckled enamel mugs we'd been using forever. It was the same ray of sun spearing my balloon valance over the kitchen window. So much routine will numb you out, it will indeed, but it was magic, of a kind – the sameness tricking you into thinking you might be young forever.

I thought he was sleeping late, late for him anyway, and I had just decided to smile about it. When I went back to our bedroom with the coffee and saw what had truly occurred, I didn't scream like a paid actress. Not one drop spilled at my hands. I set my mug, cream and real sugar, carefully down on the coaster on my side table, and I set his, cream and two Splendas, in the usual place on his side. And then I climbed back into bed.

I reached out and touched his cold lips just to make sure. I curled up and gazed at my husband for almost an hour, jealous-like – the vigil of any young lover. I was conjuring all the nice times, denying the darkness, trying to piece our lives together like a series of sunny postcards hung out on a laundry line. But even that scene was borrowed from somewhere, and the only realness I could get at was the pitch of his voice, ragged, sassing me all down the years.

I didn't make any noise in my shock because it would have disturbed my remembering. When it felt like enough time, I left him. I took my phone and tiptoed out to the screened porch, even latching the front door behind me, for privacy, before I called 911. I had to stay calm, to explain where the turnoff was; we hadn't had a road sign in ages. When I saw the red lights coming up our dirt drive, the ambulance hitting every hole and just a-bouncing so hard it would make you laugh, I went back inside to get dressed.

So now I was all alone in our house, a spacious modular Eugene had faced with composite, early on, to make it look like a log cabin. The outbuilding was small, but it was real knotty pine. It had an old-timey ladder going up to a splintery loft bed; the meager mattress and pillow were covered now by my best quilt. It took me being a widow for that place to start making me money. At the moment I had a disfigured poet staying in there. She said she was writing her memoir in verse. September was coming on well – the sunchoke and goldenrod were pooling so bright up the back slope they manufactured their own sunshine. I won't say out loud what my grown son, Gene Jr., was charging that poor creature to look out the tiny outbuilding window for inspiration. Gene Jr. and his girlfriend lived two hours away, in the city, keeping busy with jobs they could manage from home. I still found that fantastic. Since they did their careers lounging on their sofa, they had plenty of time to take care of my new business for me, photographing the outbuilding from every angle, waving their wands – now it was a *Rustic Mountain Retreat*. My view of Wadlow's Knob was on the Internet for everyone and their second cousin to gawk at, and I had strangers stacked up for months asking about roads and weather.

The kids weren't even angling for a cut of the money, yet, though if Gene Jr. ever decided to marry his young lady, you can bet those winds would commence blowing from a different direction.

At first I thought she was shy, but she only fooled me because she was short, barely reaching the wide shoulders of my son. He was bear-shaped like his daddy but chose to grow out a bushy beard. His little glasses and distracted scowl further made him his own man.

When I first looked at Gene Jr.'s girlfriend, Hana was her name, I pondered how much her hairstyle must cost. I made the journey to meet them, bringing two throw pillows I'd sewn for their sofa, in a serious fabric: Black Watch tartan. But they chose a coffee shop near their place for the big introduction. After that, it was them coming to see me.

Hana said my land was beautiful; she said it gave her a feeling of perfect serenity. My son squeezed her hand peevishly and explained how popular yoga had gotten, as though I was some shut-in who never picked up a magazine. Their schemes were in their eyes every minute. Young folks today tote the future around like draft animals, so heavy and dull. It tickled me to observe them, trying to steer their own fates.

· · ·

It was a Saturday morning, in fall, in the mountains – and shouldn't that be enough? The light was heading lavender. A breeze had blown in fresh, and today the poet had left the outbuilding, where Gene Jr. had installed a hotplate and microwave and miniature fridge for her and whoever came after. She had come into the main house to use my real stove, in my real kitchen, to bake something she was proud to show me: a loaf of quickbread using some old bananas.

I suspect she finally had cabin fever. The agreement was she could use my second bathroom to take a shower whenever she wanted. But already she'd been here one week of her two-week stay, and I had never known that to happen.

"Now, isn't this just a treat," I said, eating my slice with some apple butter I'd brought out from the pantry. The poet was having hot tea and I was enjoying a diet coke. We were gathered together on my big screened-in porch; I let her relax in my favorite glider rocker while I made do with the hard wooden one.

She was a little bit older than Gene Jr. and Hana; she might have been forty, her hair swirled up imitating an old-fashioned bun, tattoos up and down her forearms and even on her chest – all the parts not covered by her long cardigan and musty-looking leggings. She wore beat-up clogs with no socks, her heels hanging down over the soles and appearing fairly crusty. Her hot-pink scar, caused by the fire she had survived, started just under her chin and wound twice around her neck; it put me in mind of a ribbon snake. It got caught up, confused-like, in some of those chest tattoos, before trailing down towards her cleavage. I don't know where it journeyed from there.

I was raised right and knew not to stare, but I was worried about the two little boys. They had joined us on the porch that day because their mother had an errand down the road. Jordan and Caden and their mama lived in a shoddy little rental; you could just see the rusty side of it from the top of my drive.

When she dropped them off they were each toting a screen, young as they were – they were babies of nine and eight. I fixed them hot dogs and cokes, and when the mama didn't come back on time, I told the boys I had something new for them to do. Now they were sitting on the porch floor, happy as mud, going through a crazy stack of books I'd dug out of my son's childhood bedroom: his collection of *Ripley's Believe it or Not!* and *Guinness World Records*, one each to every year, big-old loud heavy things with color photos.

"Gene Jr. couldn't get enough of those, once," I said. Jordan, the older brother, was sounding out the harder words to Caden.

"I have a nephew named Aiden," said the poet, sipping her tea. Never mind the tattoos – she was prim. "I also know someone with a kid named Hayden. Or maybe it's Brayden? Ha, I don't know."

I thought about that a minute. I cleared my throat and observed that the name Jordan came before all of them, since it was from the Bible.

"Aiden, Hayden, Brayden," said the poet. "They could start their own cult."

"Now, I don't know about that," I said. I told her watching Jordan and Caden wasn't ever any trouble to me. One of them was clingy and the other had a problem with acid reflux, but they were both good boys. Sometimes they even spent the night.

I was relieved to be talking, to have a common subject, after the first week getting used to having a stranger on my property. Her sporty Subaru was parked next to my husband's old truck – my truck now – and I still startled every time I saw it. She had the Subaru covered with bumperstickers; one of them said "Coexist" in some kind of futuristic letters. Others I had to draw close to read: "Caution: This Car Makes Sudden Stops for Roadside Dance Parties."

A few times I spied her walking out to stretch herself and get a better look at Wadlow's Knob, which went up four-thousand-four-hundred feet. We were on the cold side of the mountain, bruise-blue, unmolested, nothing to interfere with the shadows here but even darker shadows – hawks circling, for one. When I first met the boys, I told Jordan, as the older brother, to mind those hawks, because a hawk would love to make a meal of their kitten.

"We don't have a kitten. We've never had a kitten. We had a hamster, but he's dead."

"What in heaven, child? I didn't get the news."

"We buried him out back. His coffin is actually a shoebox."

"Well, now. That hawk got a look at him, is what I think, and he died of fright."

I had been a teacher's aide, the times I worked, and a bit of a favorite, I don't mind saying. Patience is what I brought to it – but that was way, way back, when the only screen around was the one in the family room, letting Peter Jennings inside at six p.m.

"Evidently they do rhyme, all those names," I said now, brightly, remembering my guest was a poet. "All but Jordan." Jordan looked up from the porch floor, and I winked at him. "Tell us about y'all's fancy coincidence," I said.

"Yes, ma'am." His eyes flickered and affixed themselves to something naked; he was addressing the poet's sorry heels. "My brother and I were born the same year. But we're not twins, and we're in different grades." He turned back to the book.

"Here's how I was told," I said. "Jordan was born on New Year's Day, and their mama was pregnant with Caden only three months later. He was due the same week in January – the following year, you know. But he decided he'd come early."

"My birthday is one week before Christmas," said Caden.

"Of course it is, baby," I said. "So for two weeks out of every year," I informed the poet, "Jordan and Caden are the same age."

"Believe it or not," Jordan said, and that was a pretty moment, all four of us laughing on equal terms.

The poet said she enjoyed children but had never wanted any of her own. She said people had a hard time dealing with that – the idea of a woman choosing to be childless.

I didn't have a hard time dealing with it, though I blushed at her rudeness, speaking that way before the little boys. Why, I had heard Gene Jr. and Hana say the very same thing, indeed I had, and I sat there just a-nodding like it was the best thing they'd come up with yet.

It didn't do for one soul to push notions on another, and hadn't I learned that, almost fifty years married? Eugene and I were only in our twenties when we started out, but no babies ever came when we were young and vigorous. So we took on some foster children, here and there. All of them left our care clean as could be and well fed – and, I trust, a little more fortified with kind words than when they'd come to us.

I got attached to a few of them and longed to adopt, but my husband wanted a blood child or none at all, and at first I tried to change his mind every chance I had. But that dream proved useless, and I knew if I trapped him into it some way, those poor babies might be living in a new land of bedlam once the papers were signed. So all I could do for them after they left me was pray for their happiness.

When I was almost through with my thirties, my body suddenly felt different, but not in the way you might think. I wasn't heading for the change of life; instead it seemed I was growing younger – at least on the inside. I was full of desire, just like that, and not sure what to do with it. It came on so fast, like a cloudburst, and stayed a while, a few years.

It was a phase, you could say. Each day I found a new way to appear the fool, figuring out the schedule of the blond bagboy down at the local market – this mucky old place with concrete floors we depended on, before the chain stores came in. I'd beg use of whichever vehicle we had running and drive those rough fifteen miles to the store to buy something of no consequence, a tin of sardines or some pitiful lemon, just for the chance to wink or ask a worthless question.

Sometimes, even old as I was, I still had to link eyes with a stranger. I went to the Dollar Store to stock up for the poet's stay and got a young male cashier who appeared itchy and miserable. So I hoisted my twelve-pack of toilet paper up high and waved it in his fading face like a white flag. *Can you believe it?* I said. *I'm getting this for when the crap hits the fan.*

But during my phase of deranged lust, these urges were constant. I couldn't shake myself free of them. The principal at the elementary school back then, my boss, he was a dirty old muskrat with false teeth, but that didn't stop me from asking him what kind of trouble he'd got into over the weekend. At that time in my life, I needed to be ridiculous every minute. *You old hellraiser,* I would call down the hall, ducking into the restroom after, to examine my face in my compact mirror.

I was the one nudging Eugene awake of a night, and you'd think a big beefy man would have appreciated a frisky wife. But his job took a toll, and mostly he just seemed confused. It wasn't like me to be so urgent, not about anything, and least of all that.

And so, with nothing in that bed done any different from what had been done before, I fell pregnant, for the first time and the last, and when I told Eugene about his triumph, he didn't act like they do on TV or in the movies. He didn't rage at me or commence weeping with gratitude. He said nothing at all for a terrible, long moment. Then he said, "We're no spring chickens, but I imagine we'll do all right."

Once the baby was born, a big-old boy weighing nine pounds, I stayed home, isolated with little Gene Jr. That was a situation my friends and sisters-in-law, whose children were older by then, in school seven hours a day or even grown, took care to warn me about. They told me being alone all day with a baby would drive me out of my head. Oh, they were full of themselves and their own stories, driving up to visit, loading me down with all their cast-off baby-boy clothes and squawking like ravens. They couldn't wait to observe my suffering.

But for me, it wasn't like that at all. It was the opposite of what-all they said – it was the best time I ever had. Sometimes lately, in my night dreams, I could still feel the weight of my sweet baby boy making my hip and shoulder ache. We went around intertwined, in those years, our faces melded right at the cheek, while I did my housework. That warm, tender head pinned me down to earth. I was obliged to guard that bundle, and he was all heaviness. He was the pride of my life.

Then the dream would go bad, and the cherub baby would shrivel in my arms, turn into a mouse or a little lizard. I would drop the changeling in my kitchen sink and scream *no, stop*, watching it swirl down the drain. When I woke up it was from my own shout, the bed so empty I found myself scratching around in it like a wild animal, looking for something to hold and not sure who I was missing.

"There was a time," I told the poet, "when I thought I'd be childless, too. But the Lord finally blessed me with a wonderful son."

She nodded stiffly and turned her eyes to her tea. Meanwhile Jordan and Caden had found the section in the book called *Human Oddities*, and they were growing more lively.

I knew the pictures well and could not be shocked by them anymore: the stout foreign fella who pulled a whole car down a track, using only hooks in his back; the lanky boy from the Midwest who dislocated his jaw to stuff in a record number of drinking straws; the world's tallest man ever, who died from an infection in his leg he couldn't reach down to tend; the fattest woman, toted out to her grave by workers who usually moved grand pianos; the glamorous lady with the frightening fingernails, grown out so long they swirled down to the ground.

The sight of those fingernails used to leave me stressed – I would finally catch myself grinding my teeth. I just never understood it, me who couldn't grow out nails enough to make a decent back scratcher. How had she ever done it? How did she manage her day?

The boys punched at the pages. "Epic," one of them said. "Awww – that is *dis*-gusting."

I blushed again, afraid the poet would get her feelings hurt, since she herself was a human oddity. "Let me hold that book a minute, Jordan," I said, and he gave it to me, "yes ma'am," with an irritated glance. I flipped to something safer, the section on space facts, and read aloud to them all like a real teacher: *A day on Saturn is only 10 hours long, but a year on Saturn is the same as 29 years on Earth … Without Earth's gravity, we would float off the planet. If you kicked a ball, it would fly forever … The number of stars in the known universe cannot be counted …*

The poet knew a thing or two about space and stars, so at last she arrived for the conversation. She talked about visiting a famous observatory, the year she lived in Arizona, and said she was able to draw up a person's natal chart and study it for the interpretations, though you couldn't get any money for that anymore, now that websites offered the same service free of charge.

That reminded me of Gene Jr.'s college education, him going away four years to State and coming back from Raleigh so smooth, his tone drier, a veil of polish over his already serious nature. "Bright as anything – he got a scholarship for the tuition part," I said, wishing I hadn't sighed.

No matter what their specialty was, all the folks on the covers of the Ripley's and Guinness books seemed to have their limbs sprung wide or their eyes popped out. Strewn around like they were, all over the screened-porch floor, they made a person feel outnumbered. "Like the circus watching *you*," I said.

"I beg your pardon?" said the poet.

They weren't at all cheap, those books, if my memory still served me at seventy-five. They were hardback; they'd cost dear. "When you have only one child," I told her low, "you can do more for them."

The poet liked to trace her loop of burn scar with her index finger as she talked. I could tell it settled her.

When I was her age, with a husband to tend to and a little one in the house, it made me so mad to be sick or hurt. I didn't have time for it, and my weakness embarrassed me. But now that I was old and alone and wasn't obliged to carry on with all the housework and all the nurturing like nothing whatsoever was wrong, I almost took pleasure in my aching body, the little disasters of old age. My sore joints were like my children – I greeted them, of a morning – and one time, I ripped open the papery skin of my forearm on the screen-door latch, a fantastic cut that got infected. It deepened and spread, so out of proportion to the incident it would make you chuckle, and eventually, after the worst pain subsided, I couldn't stop messing with it, poking beneath the bandage my doctor had set for me. That sore of mine kept changing colors, and it took forever to go away – I kept a jealous eye on it, like my own private sunset. The poet would say I had manifested it.

But all those dire things that had taken my friends and kin – the heart disease and the lung disease and the variety of female cancers – so far, I had strictly denied them. "Nothing wrong with me the occasional aspirin and a little company can't cure," I joked to the poet, some days later. I was on my knees, pruning the creeper that was curling into the big A/C unit in back of my house.

It had turned humid again, her last week, and since the outbuilding didn't have air conditioning – I would have to ask Gene Jr. to install a window box, next summer – she was with me more, and asking all kinds of questions. She complained that the Wi-Fi this week had turned spotty, although Jordan and Caden, who were in my living room enjoying some sandwiches I'd made them, banana with Marshmallow Creme, seemed to be having no trouble with their little screens. It was true they had spent a night or two, coming to me with their little backpacks stuffed full. Their mama was off somewhere – helping her best friend, she said, who had man trouble.

That's when the poet fell to whispering. She talked about meth and about the *Rural Opioid Crisis* – she rolled it out just like a headline – but I stood my ground. If the best friend with man trouble was drug-addled and not merely heartbroken, it wasn't my place to judge.

The poet nudged me to remember how many times I'd been left to care for Jordan and Caden like an unpaid grandmother. Oh, she was getting nosy, she was indeed, and at first I tried to change the subject, to save her mood and mine. That's just manners.

I asked her how she liked my Joseph's Coat climbers, glowing so holy in their pink and yellow – the prettiest things I had left. My husband had started my roses for me ages ago, and then he tended them so well one of the blooms got a first-place ribbon, down at the regional fair; I don't recall which year.

But I do remember the summer before he planted the roses. One afternoon, Eugene had put on his Rough Rider gloves and pulled up my entire vegetable garden, roots and all. It had to be done, he said, and acted sad about it. My tomatoes that year weren't so good, but I knew plain well that blight didn't hop from one kind of plant to another, as he would have me believe.

I don't remember anymore why he did it, except I didn't please him, somehow, and a dark mood took him over. You get good at not-remembering some things, if you care to keep living. Growing me the fancy roses was how he apologized. He let me claim that prize ribbon as my own doing, and not a soul was the wiser.

The poet just stood there, with her tea, looming over me bored-like, gazing up at the scenery. I told her the story of my ruined vegetable garden, though I blushed to do it, even all these years later. Exposing Eugene, I felt a bang of ice. It was like tripping over a root – not knowing how close you are to the edge of the mountain.

Now, though, she would tell me all about her scar. I figured fair was fair.

But she wouldn't tell it, quite. I guess she thought me too frail, or too daft, to handle a young woman's horror story. It wasn't true. In my life, I had seen and heard plenty. There was a child in this very county who'd been found stowed in a closet, when he didn't develop as nicely as his older brothers and sisters. My own daddy used to brain our pet cats with shovels, no hesitation, if they turned up with distemper.

She started to tell me, but held back, that mote of pride still her own. Instead, she divulged the rest of her life, which proved an interesting mess. She said she enjoyed younger men and that her friends called her a cougar, but whenever she fell in love with a woman, they were usually close to her own age. She said she had a famous brother who was a recovering alcoholic and a recovering porn addict, both, but also a brilliant prop stylist. I didn't dare ask what that was.

He posted pictures from around the world, she said. He posted updates about keeping clean. He, too, was writing a memoir. He probably had more than fifty thousand followers on Instagram.

"What that means, in modern lingo, is that he's no longer just a micro-influencer."

"Well, now," I said, "think of that." Folks today, they don't consider anything a sin except a secret.

You needed a vehicle with four-wheel drive to make it up to my house, so Gene Jr. and Hana were obliged to park their electric car at the bottom of the road and hike up on foot. I happened to look out my kitchen window and saw them rounding the last corner, trudging, and I hustled outside to yell *hey* and waved like a little old cheerleader with a pompom, so I wouldn't appear surprised. My son had texted me they were planning a visit, but that was days ago now, and I didn't like to admit how often I lost my phone.

"You lose your phone again, Mom?" Gene cut a look at his girl after receiving my hug.

"Now, let's start off right," I said. "Who needs a cold drink?"

But they'd brought a six pack of their own special beer, the fancy craft kind priced so high it was once a great joke, between my husband and me. *Let's start us up our own brewery, Mother,* Eugene used to say. *We'll get Junior to run it.*

They were unusually restless, even for them; they wouldn't sit on the porch and have a proper visit. Gene Jr. went immediately to the outbuilding like he had business there, and his girl joined me in the kitchen, where I'd been arranging family photos on my sewing table. I meant to go to town and get a scrapbook on clearance, the next time I drove off the mountain.

That day had started with me hauling some of Gene Jr.'s old metal Tonka trucks out of the crawl space beneath the house and handing one each to Jordan and Caden, who were still with me. If I couldn't find my phone, I could tell them their mama was still calling to ask about them, and there was half a chance it wouldn't be a lie.

I'd given the boys firm instructions not to fall on the trucks' sharp edges, nor to go further up Wadlow's Knob than I could keep track of them. *Make sure this old lady can still hear you.* I'd handed them my garden trowel and a wooden spoon and they had scrambled away as far as the hard green laurel thicket at the end of my sightline and commenced digging.

The spectacle of the little boys toting those old trucks did mischief to my memory. It threatened to undo me, and that's when I got out all the old photos to steady myself, sorting out which year was which.

"Look at this one," I said now, handing Hana a snapshot of a little Gene Jr. in a fuzzy dragon costume. "I made that for him for his third birthday. He wore it to bed, wouldn't let me wash it."

"Aww," said Hana. She stopped fingering her shining hair. "That is so cute." I offered her my chair, but she shook her head and stayed standing.

The wind carried the brothers' voices to us. The older one was bossing the younger one, but they were having a big time of it, you could tell. I cleared my throat. "Well, Miss Hana. How have y'all been? Any news from town?"

"Hmm?" she said. "No." She gave me back the photo. "I mean, not really. Just busy-busy. Life is good." She and Gene, they'd come to check up on me – just to check in, she said quickly, and to settle up with the poet. Make sure everything was okay.

After I'd had a few guests, they wouldn't need to do this anymore, she promised. Once I got in a routine with the vacation rental and all.

She eyed me tartly. "So, I have to ask. I mean … we wanted to know, were you comfortable with having a performance artist around? I know she's quite the flamboyant character."

I pictured the poet, going cold whenever I mentioned our Lord. Stirring her tea so nervous and neat, with no call for that, since she didn't take sweetener. "Performance artist? I thought she was supposed to be a writer. I thought she was in there working on her writing."

"Oh, she was," said Hana.

"She kept worrying me about her connection. I wondered why she would have to be on the Internet, anyway, just to write a memoir."

But I had so much to learn. Young folks today, they didn't do one thing. They did everything. Hana revealed to me that the poet also happened to be a fire twirler. She performed at festivals; people came to watch her throw around flaming things. It was her *passion*, said Hana. She played with fire on purpose.

Finally, I had my story. The poet got burned, Hana told me, because her spotter had failed her. I could see I needed to know what a spotter was. And on top of that, the overhead clearance for the stage had been misrepresented – she was suing the venue for that – it was a complete outrage. One of the poet's pois had gotten wrapped around her neck, Hana explained. She couldn't get it off her in time.

Later, I booted up my fickle old machine and typed Hana's nonsense into a search engine. It was true – it had been in the local news, last year, but evidently I had missed it all. When Hana said *pois*, I heard *poise*, which made more sense, the way I viewed the poet.

During the telling, I kept quiet. My hand crept up to my neck. I was shaken, but this girl need not hear of it.

Fire twirling! I couldn't see it for anything. My guest had been two weeks on my property, and she had never once smiled. The long-gone circus of my early youth, bumping through the hills, setting up in this or that vacant field – those acrobats were always done up in grimacing face paint, to match the clowns.

"I guess everyone needs their blaze of glory, don't they?" I turned tactfully away and went to work up some dishes in the sink, adding, "I'm obliged for the information, Hana." I flipped the faucet up steaming hot so she would know to leave.

I fell to daydreaming. I imagined the house on fire, the secret ways I would find to get out, and somehow they changed places, like twins, Gene Jr. coming in to me and his girl disappearing down the hall.

"Hey, mama."

I turned to him. Unexpectedly, there at my kitchen window, the same old sun washing in, my grown child wrapped me in a fierce bear hug. I wouldn't cry, but I clung to him, inhaled deep of his neck. The sweet smell had never yet changed.

"Why, thank you, baby," I said. He released me. I peered into those strange little glasses of his to see what was coming.

75

"We really need you to be more careful," said Gene Jr. "We need to know that you're staying safe."

"I'm perfectly well, son," I said. "What in heaven are you fishing after?"

"We need you to be more careful about who you trust." His mouth was a straight line drawn in that beard. He took me gently by the shoulders, so frustrated to know my mind – he was nothing like his daddy had been at all.

"Her lifestyle sounds strange," I said. "But she minded herself, mostly. We've been fine."

He wasn't talking about the poet, though; he was intent on the children. It seemed the poet had texted him all about Jordan and Caden. She had called it a serious situation, and Gene Jr. had been made to investigate.

Now he was telling me he'd contacted CPS and that I should expect a visit from a social worker soon, someone who would take the little boys into custody now that their mother was God knows where, looking after her habit.

I reached down to worry a twinge in my leg. "Not coming back, then? I never saw that in her."

He closed his eyes. "Of course you didn't."

I left him standing there and went into the living room, where I picked up a nice fat sofa cushion and gave it a squeeze. "Well, then."

"Well what, mama?"

"Well, nothing. Lord Jesus!" I pushed the cushion into my forehead, right at the brain, trying to work up a timeline. "Mercy, child," I said. "Give them a day more to hide, at least."

Bad Tooth Brandon

For a few years, a weird number of Brandons were known around town. Four of them there were, all around the same age. The town was hovering on top of its own rustic charm – too big to be small, now, but not big enough. Not big enough to stop us forever running into our shaky selves.

With that last name he had, Brandon Shoemaker should have been a cobbler, or at least a woodworker. But the millennium was still new – no maker culture around yet. The only ones going in for craft were the faded first-line hippies.

Instead, Brandon Shoemaker was a bouncer who worked at the one bar downtown sketchy enough to require a bouncer. He distinguished himself by his silence; also, he was tall and thick enough to flirt with giantism. He stooped sadly; his head hung between his shoulders like a spent cannonball.

He smoked menthol American Spirits whose butts he discarded on the town's broken brick sidewalks, though he would have swung at anyone else for desecrating antiques. He was a collector of vintage Big and Tall peacoats and old watches.

Brandon Shoemaker had had a sweetheart, a Libertarian from out in the county, a little snake-faced guy who had joined the Army in a great blaze of passion after 9/11 and come back from the desert recognizing no one, his brain injury not from combat but from an ordnance accident on base.

Left alone then, and not inclined to move on, Shoemaker calcified into an eccentric. He didn't stay with anybody. He was sometimes seen in the cemetery down by the river road. A few famous authors were buried there, in a section popular with tourists.

The next Brandon, Brandon Cullen, I heard about more than I ever saw. My big sister Kells pointed him out to me, using this hoarse stage whisper that was pretty much her real voice. We spotted Brandon Cullen hurrying out of Home Depot one day in high summer, shouldering a load of freshly sawed planks.

Kells had been with Brandon Cullen one night; she had found him quite vain. "Here's the truth, doll: he fucks like he's looking into a mirror," she told me. That was her vulgar-dainty way. Brandon Cullen had climbed out of these eastern hills on his snowboarding talent and was busy getting sponsored out in Colorado – "*real* mountains," went the snobbish report; "*real* snow." Had he actually said it?

He only came back home to see his parents, who owned a big house in the fine area of town, and, an hour or so further north, among the highest peaks, thirty acres they were hoping to sell to developers. But it was rumored that Brandon Cullen was building a terrain park on that same lonely mountain, where up-and-coming snowboarders could train.

It never stayed winter for long, though. By the end of February, in town, the crocus were up. We were hardly the Rockies: we were older and closer. Nothing regal at all – God, we were as suffused in reproach as a mother's hug.

Then there was Brandon Smith – he moved away, too, to Atlanta first. The further he got from us, the larger he bloomed. Naturally Kells had been with this Brandon, too. Word of his success began trickling up the mountain; she boosted their intimacy a notch by calling him her ex-boyfriend.

Brandon Smith's new name was DJ Indelicate, and eventually the South could not hold him anymore and he moved to the west coast. Indelicate became associated with Portland, where he and some friends operated a production studio, and with San Francisco. He toured in Brazil; he became massive in Argentina. He filled up clubs in the UK and Germany. He lived for a while in Amsterdam. A decade or so later, he had a Wiki page.

One day, his original name resurfaced in an op-ed essay for the digital branch of a giant newspaper. Someone had given the piece a leggy title: "Growing Up African American in Appalachia: Cultural Perspective From an International Tastemaker."

Posting the link to Facebook, Kells gushed: "OMG pinch me y'all it's Brandon Smith we knew him when right?!"

By then, Kells had another life. She was raising two children, homeschooling them in this suite of junk RVs rigged up on a riverbank in Spivey Cove, which backed up to Spivey Mountain. It was her project with a couple of other single girlfriends and their kids. They liked to call it a co-op.

Kells and I, we had the same mother, but with our different fathers who were only ghosts, the outcome was like a miracle: a family that only produced daughters. My little nieces were garrulous, untamed; their wild hair had never been cut. Already they had the air of carrying on tradition.

The fourth Brandon was Brandon Haggerty, and he sat on a king's throne. If Brandon Shoemaker was the loner and Brandon Cullen was the rich kid and Brandon Smith was the star, then Brandon Haggerty was the savior. I mean, we all got a piece. He had absurd gold curls like the Cowardly Lion – after he gets made over in Oz – but also a blissed-out melancholy like Aslan, after the White Witch of Narnia slays him on the stone table.

Birch and Petal knew these characters intimately. Despite what else you could say about her, Kells read her daughters the classics. But way before my nieces were born, I had landed on the likeness.

"Brandon Haggerty likes to shake that big old mane of his," I announced to my sister one bitter morning. "Are you going to let him get away with that?" During the height of the Brandon Era, you had to say their whole names. Distinguishing the Brandons became as automatic as cursing the rents, which had, by then, begun a dispiriting climb.

Brandon Haggerty picked up landscaping jobs in season and had the aura of a hardwood mountain on Christmas morning:

pure glory, but with all the green gone. He was a regular at the bar, and he didn't miss a house party. He could be found on any front porch where an old-time or country-blues jam was tuning up, toting his mandolin like some medically fragile baby.

Brandon Haggerty didn't go in for the garage-rock surge of the early 2000s, or for any genre of music after 1940, really. For him, it was Pre-War only. The ancient ballads, the endlessly circling traditionals: *Soldier's Joy, Whiskey Before Breakfast, Bonaparte's Retreat*. His instrument was expensive; it was rumored that he really lived on a trust fund, and that his mother, a native of Charlotte, was heir to the Lance Crackers fortune.

"Haggerty is supersonic," said Kells. "Haggerty is a stud. You better believe he knows it, doll."

Besides her being six years older and full of grapevine intelligence, this was the other difference between us: she wouldn't throw a person away after stumbling on their stupid side. Secrets, weakness – they could not undo her. She sold weed to get by and knew how to make her own salad dressing, and when I didn't know any better than to find real jobs, jobs on the books, to make my part of the bills, she had a pot of good coffee ready for me every morning.

She got up with me no matter what. At that time we were sharing a flat in one of the three-storey stone buildings near downtown, the ones they'd built in the 1920s for tuberculosis patients. Renovation wasn't here yet – not quite. We were inhabiting the last days.

The old steam radiators fussed and banged like player pianos in a haunted church, intent on professing the word. The one working burner on the narrow gas stove did its part to help the kitchen seem warm.

Even inside, Kells always wore this wool beanie with alpacas stitched on it. She pushed up the sleeves of her baggy cardigan and scratched her arms with ravaged fingernails, digging and digging. She called me "crazy-adorable" – I was elfin but bland, one of the lesser mushrooms – and she noted every piece of my outfit: a denim dress with cable tights and little ankle boots, my secondhand fuchsia swing coat that looked like a cape, hood and all. That winter, I was working as an administrative assistant in a busy massage therapist's office.

Years later, holding several degrees, I would become a therapist myself. But I worked on psyches, never terrible flesh. I didn't like bodies, and tended to avoid them. Back then, bare bodies offered vulnerably to professionals seemed the most worrisome of all.

We were free to talk about Brandon Haggerty because he was gone. Kells had shown him out the door that morning with a long hug and a kick with her bluish bare foot to the seat of his cargo pants, and from the tall grimy window in the front room we watched him walk down the building's broken steps, whistling. He was sandwiched by his two dogs, Lacey and Shakespeare. He passed the stone gargoyles on the second stoop nearer the street and tapped the more crumbling one on its head, the side with no ear, and got into his Dodge, this large barking truck from the early '80s with the original ram hood ornament, and drove away.

Kells smiled more than anyone I ever knew. Her smile was wide and loose and ringed in the old style of fillings. She flashed all that metal around like a parlor trick. Earlier in the week, she had fussed at me because I wouldn't go out for a beer with her the very night I turned legal. Now I was twenty-one years old plus four days. The momentum was gone, and along with it the cash.

Christmas was two weeks away. We had to decide if we were going to figure out presents to send to our mother and all of our aunts, or else get the car we shared into the garage for transmission work. It was a Corolla, the oldest kind of Corolla where the front grille looked like a face.

My sister put on a pair of men's long underwear and men's socks and then these ugly work boots she had, real boots with steel toes. She poured both our cups of coffee into a camping thermos that she handed to me. She found her keys under her white iron bed, and, for the drama of it, wrapped herself head to toe in her favorite quilt and drove me to work.

"Let's see if I can get you there without putting this beast into reverse," she said, muffled inside her quilt robe, and in this way we reached downtown. She let the car go full skid, surrendering to the ice, looping around the one-way streets to avoid a tight spot. We whooped until the car shook, and she eased up next to the curb with a long crunch. "Bye, Little Bit," she said, throwing me a kiss, and I got back out into the wavering cold.

The hills visible between the buildings had that glow. Rosy but ruined. It needed to be sunny for that, and also well below freezing, and also a day in December. It had to be this part of the world. In the future, I would see plenty of higher, sharper mountains, the jagged snowcapped kind, in my own country and in other people's countries, too. But I never ran into that particular tragic-glad light, the glow that could drive you to pray, even if no one had thought to raise you that way.

My boss, the massage therapist, he was a muscular middle-aged man who was tanned year round. He made me nervous, though he never made a move to touch me. In fact, when he addressed me, asked me to do this or that, he had a habit of keeping his arms completely behind his back, hands clasped. It was courtly, this gesture, but I didn't like it. He looked like a soul who might beg to be wheeled around, even if all his limbs worked.

I tended to be timid, but I wasn't any virgin. More than once, I let one of Brandon Haggerty's musician friends, this young guy, a twenty-year-old clawhammer-banjo player, creep inside the sleeping bag I kept on top of my mattress on the floor. My bedroom was at the back, the coldest room in the flat.

He was only a boy, that scrawny picker, but he was already losing his hair. He was haunted by a family he complained about constantly, in this admiring whine, dropping their names in every phrase like you were supposed to know who was who, who to like and who to hate, whose bad behavior could never be stopped, and who was getting ready to fall down and die.

He was profoundly distracted, which freed me up, since I couldn't always be glad to see him. Before sex, he rambled on and on in that rapid, back-country twang, a near falsetto, sounding like some sweet old man. He only looked at me sharp once the lights were out.

• • •

Being December, the sun was down by five, and Kells met me just as I came out of the massage therapist's office. The car had died while I was at work, she told me, without a speck of worry. "Old Bessie shit the bed," she said, so I could giggle about it.

She had walked downtown to retrieve me, dressed now in a green velvet bustier and jeans, her waist-length hair plaited like a milkmaid. She wore glittering eyeshadow and a man's Carhartt coat that matched the work boots. She'd hustled some cash in the hours since she'd last seen me, and so we walked here and there. She bought me a pizza slice and a cupcake, and then we went down to the bar, the one where Brandon Shoemaker worked. His face, it was stony and livid as ever.

"Hey, Sexy," Kells rasped at him, scratching inside her mittens. She was always the bravest creature in town. "Guess who's twenty-one now?" she said.

Big Brandon Shoemaker dipped his head away from the collar of that Navy-issue peacoat, boring his eyes into the driver's license I offered up to him. He wore a cloudy old Timex, the kind with the springy metal band. It was stretched to its limit and his wrist showed through, bellicose with hair. In that buried voice he had, Brandon Shoemaker said something about a belated happy birthday. He called me "Sis," which made Kells happy as hell.

Nothing about the night foretold chaos. There was Brandon Haggerty, in his usual place in the back, on a dumpy old couch by the dartboard. He, too, formed a single portrait: filmy blue eyes and affable to eternity. He was lazy – he could stay in that same position for hours. Kells sat on his knee a second, but she always had to be moving, and soon enough she wandered away. I lost track of them both, eventually, and ended up on the covered back deck clutching my third legal beer, this dark solid thing, talking nonsense to a total stranger.

Something about his urgency, that and an unpleasant accent – from the north, pinched and claustrophobic with information – might have warned me. But for the moment, he had me where he wanted. He pitched his intent to reach me under the evil odor of a kerosene space heater.

"You look young for twenty-one," he said.

I twirled around a couple times, to make my cape stand out.

"That's a good way to get vertigo," he said.

So I did it again.

He said: "I turned twenty-five on Halloween. I've got a Halloween birthday."

"You're probably more like thirty," I said, twirling away so I could blush for him.

That was the end of the night, in my memory. They found me in time, but he had ripped my hood, yanking it. Brandon Shoemaker, who was an intellectual, argued with the cops about how to properly spell out *Rohypnol*. Incompetence incensed him, including his own, and during the whole ordeal, he had actually foamed at the mouth, Kells reported. But it was Brandon Haggerty who planned what had to be done.

After he helped my sister get me home to my bed, Brandon Haggerty went back out into that ten-degree night and met Brandon Shoemaker getting off work. I liked to picture how they muttered it out – it would be Brandon Haggerty doing most of the convincing, and Brandon Shoemaker, tough as he was, sliding under the spell of that soft-voiced bright lion.

Together, the Brandons combed downtown, in and out of alleys, widening the circle, this house party and that one, until they found the stranger. Together they broke his arm.

But in the year following the incident, Brandon Haggerty began to shrink. The decline was slow at first, then outrageous. His hair got so dirty and complicated he cut it off. His grin turned into an apology. One day, a side tooth was gone, and the tooth's nearest neighbor was showing clear signs of defeat.

So he took a firmer grip on his mandolin and talked some friends into forming a four-piece band. Brandon Haggerty could sing a little, so he was the natural leader; he called his band Bad Tooth Brandon and the Haymakers. Kells called herself their manager. They played a few festivals, up and down and under the escarpment, and over into the Piedmont, but it didn't go far past the first year.

Kells lied at first, told me that the tooth had been injured that night, the night of the incident, in the fight to avenge me. Later, though, after Brandon Haggerty died of an overdose, and I was the only one who couldn't believe it, I learned about the undertow of all their free time, my sister, her lover – about what it meant, about so much I had never realized, me living in my own owlish head, saving my wages, walking breathlessly up the steep river road on my days off to find flashes of quartz, brainstorming a future that didn't depend on scraps.

They named a drink after him, at the bar: The Haggerita. But the thing was, he was never really a drinker. My innocence – Kells had nursed it like a terrarium. I was like some pet salamander she had kept impervious to the real climate, stroking my soft backbone, closing me off under glass.

To get free, I had to move far away. I filled out the forms, I got the aid, and I went to college, where I planned my own courses. Except once my nieces were born, I had to come back to visit.

If you knew the right people, life appeared to go on, even unfolding sweetly, as though fate had a real job. The years stopped feeling new, they only accumulated, and this was true: Kells stayed clean. She had claimed her piece of the valley. She had the best trailer of the bunch, a vintage Airstream some old-man admirer had sold her for a song. It only seemed natural that all the Brandons were gone now, far away or dead. Shoemaker killed himself with a shotgun, one foggy dawn next to his true love's grave, and if no one had written a song about it yet, it only wanted time, the particular voice.

Kells made curtains for the Airstream from the quilt she'd once worn. And when craft came back in big, she was right there on top of it, turning her talent into honest money. She wrote, "Hi there! I'm a self-taught fiber artist, and except for this blog, I pretty much live off the grid."

Sometimes fall in my old town would stretch into late November – a weird half-season strung out in warmth. One visit I recall, it was gold. I watched Birch, Kells' dark-haired daughter, the one they said looked like me, trying to nurse a Carolina wren. She'd discovered it hobbling around in the litter of yellow poplar leaves on the riverbank, and was contriving a nest for it out of a coffee mug and a hole-filled washcloth. Petal was the younger one, a curly-haired blonde.

The girls were happy to see me – that was the thing to keep. Spivey Mountain rose behind them, gloomy as a father, and they shrieked out their love. "This bird has been hurt," said Petal, sounding glad for the opportunity.

Confederate Jasmine

Her eighteenth birthday would fall on Easter Sunday – only one more week to worry about anyone stopping them. Easter was eighteen was freedom.

"Has that ever happened before?" Nehemiah asked Esmé, whacking her on the front of her olive-drab jacket with the back of his hand – respectfully, though, on the collar, not the chest, trying to keep her alert while he drove. His hands were long and wonderfully made, graceful, even feminine; he'd played piano starting around age five, and his old parents (he was the far last of five siblings) had thought him a prodigy.

Sweet characters, both of them, but hardly part of his life. Dad was alive but gone as fuck. Mom had gotten ovarian cancer. She had helped herself along with alternative cures until the social worker had forced her to get real medical help, for the sake of her younger children. "Younger children" meant Nehemiah, mostly; she had faced down her terror of Western medicine, gotten radiation to stay alive just for him. Hadn't worked a bit – it was just too late – but the knowledge of what she'd done, that's where he got his two or three shreds of confidence.

She hadn't lived long enough to see what real piano prodigies were, playing for their hundreds of thousands of fans on YouTube. You had to be three years old to really be a prodigy. Two was better.

"Has that ever happened before?" he repeated. "Your birthday falling on Easter? Hey, now. Has that ever happened?" On and on, up the scale of randomness.

He thought he might buy Esmé a little Easter basket for her birthday, pick up some cheap China-made thing at the dollar store and beautify it with Spanish moss, get a cupcake at a bakery and tuck it down in there, too: a little nest. Maybe hustle up a birthday candle for the cupcake. He'd been telling her how awesome Spanish moss was for so long – the time had come to prove it.

His ragged nails made contact with the trinity of political buttons she had pinned to the lapel of her olive-drab jacket.

Silence Equals Violence.
Stand Up For Science.
RESIST!

She was always saying she wanted to be a journalist.

"Yo-yo-yo," he whisper-shouted at her, though no one in the universe could hear him. "Let's get those eyes open."

He moved his hand around, tried a different position, continued tapping Esmé's plastic buttons with his fingertips, making a little beat of it, like an army of rodents on a tile floor after midnight, going after a nub of cheese. ("Battle with the Mouse King" from the *Nutcracker*. *Carnival of the Animals*, played *andantino*: slightly faster than slow. The reason he'd gotten so good, way back when, was because no one had nagged him to practice. It was also the reason he'd quit.)

"Come on, Esmé."

She had nodded off in the passenger seat of the van they'd named Zelda, after the video game. The Wind Waker Zelda.

He was having trouble staying awake himself, but not for the same reason as Esmé. For him, it was mostly fatigue and worry and whatever toxic exhaust this shit-heap vehicle was surely leaking into his brain cells, putting his intelligence to rest atom by atom.

But he could do this. Everything in him was made to keep on going. He was leading this adventure, but he didn't have the power to stop it.

His destination was a shining southern beach, the Atlantic curling over a stage of white sand day and night without ceasing. The way he remembered it, you reached this beach down a road where a bunch of appalling trees held their own weight aloft, like soldiers. *Conquistadors*. Spanish moss hung all in them – the veil that hid the good world from the bad. Live oaks. But the moss looked dead.

This beach, it was stuck in his head from the family vacation. It was the one family vacation that had ever happened. His brothers and sisters teased him that he'd been a toddler, too young to actually remember the trip. But he did; he did remember. A scorching light, like high noon but at dawn. Diamonds jumping on top of the water, the waves crashing insanely. Someone's hands clutching him close, all the delirious voices miles above his head, climbing up to join the wind. Happiness? It was about being on fire, and nothing less. He remembered his mother singing to him at home, making up words for wordless songs.

Sleee-eep, Little Man. Here's your bear. Here's your fan. For years, for him, those were the opening bars of *Clair de Lune*. Even if it was possible he had made up the words himself, teaching himself to play the song one day, the voice was surely hers, and the ghost of comfort.

This van, though, it was an old Econoline from the '80s, and it smelled like the layers of an old man's ass – some combination of an idiot cigarette habit and urine-colored liquor like gasoline that would pickle your guts and sag your face into savagery with exploding red veins. It was the smell of no hope at all. And yet, even from guys who looked and smelled like that, the expectation of praise, of admiration over nothing. Unbelievable.

Chicken Don, the man who'd sold him the van, he was supposed to be a family friend. A real Renaissance man, was he – his musty, bleak jokes covered all the bases: secret whores and surprise syphilis, pedophile priests and dicks speared on stakes, an impotent emperor, as though emperors still mattered. No one got out whole.

After you coughed up your fake laugh at the end of each joke, you were then supposed to get serious the second the old fuckface got serious, stay on key for the interminable storytelling bound to come. Chicken Don: salt of the earth, puffed up on his low-level weed empire and not wanting legalization ever to come to their state, Nehemiah figured, because then wouldn't all his sleazy backwoods aristocracy become the real joke?

Chicken Don, his arrogance was just a mudslide, nothing noble under there at all. *Did I ever tell you about the time my best buddy and I drove to San Francisco in one haul? Traded off driving and pissed in Mason jars so we wouldn't have to stop except for gas. The jars without the hootch in it, that is. Ha! Ha! Taking turns with this chick in the back. Little pig was passed out cold. Pretty, though. And we made it. Didn't stop till we saw the Golden Gate Bridge. Let me tell ya, if you've never seen the sun rise over the Golden Gate Bridge, you haven't lived. And then she woke up, and I told her, you're dead, baby, but don't worry, right here is Heaven. Ha. Ha.*

Old Chicken Don, doing his scabby growing thing on a few backwoods acres, the land populated with a bunch of depressed farm animals – poultry, naturally, but also a bonafide mule and four Nubian Pygmy goats named after the Beatles. No Internet for a long time because he thought they were watching him, but somehow, nonetheless, there he was with that mail-order bride or whoever she happened to be, lurking around the corners of his dirty old house, tidying up. Probably spoke no English, but who could tell, since she never did speak? Scared to death.

The situation made Nehemiah want to kill someone. When he had to consider himself, who Nehemiah really was, he decided he was rough, sure, but also, he understood almost everything.

A survivor, for real. A survivalist, really – but not the redneck-dickhead type of survivalist like Chicken Don.

For instance, his first girlfriend still loved him, and that meant something. Still wanted him, even. She was older, in fact she was four years older, but she said Nehemiah was the best she had ever had. She moaned vaguely of being broke, told him she missed him, texted him a pic of herself with the latest guy she was fucking, to make him jealous.

It was nothing but an anonymous closeup, girl on top, a clueless cock shoved into a vacant pussy. It could be any two people, both of their groins shaved, but he recognized her tank top with the ripped black lace along the bottom hem. If it was hot, it was also gruesome. A punchline. Those squirming genitals, they looked like one naked mole rat devouring the other in a mutual honor killing. (He figured it wasn't Mom who had taught him to read; he had really learned it himself, burrowing through Dad's ceiling-high stacks of *National Geographic*s that someone later called a fire hazard. The proof was in the random shit he remembered: naked mole rats had no ability to feel pain. It was male seahorses who carried the babies.)

I like it that you don't shave, he'd told Esmé, over and over, and especially in the soft, nervous minutes before he'd removed her virginity. *I like it. It's more natural.* She was shaky but ready, had taken off all her clothes except these arm warmers she liked to wear that were black and red, artfully ripped like some attempt at punk rock. *They're all wartorn*, she said fretfully. *They look like bloody bandages, am I right?* She had put those frilly arms around his long, naked, bony back as he began a barely perceptible pumping – the slow release off a long sustain pedal. *I like your bloody bandages*, he'd muttered, stroking her pink hair back from her forehead.

Standing there listening to Chicken Don's stories, Nehemiah's own head bobbed along like a metronome. He pictured shutting the old fucker up once and for all with a jackknife to the scrotum – one twist to the left, another to the right – and watching him bleed out into that little sewage trickle he called a creek.

But how would a person even find the ball sac in the vast crotch tent of those filthy Carhartt overalls? His enormous stomach was stuffed down in there, too. Probably the entire Satanic mess had begun to fuse together.

"I used to build cabinets with your Daddy," said Chicken Don for approximately the six hundredth and sixty-sixth time. "Real wood. Maple. Not this particle-board shit you see everywhere. I first met you when you were two years old." He put up two fingers and cackled at the accidental peace sign. He was done loading Nehemiah and Esmé down with the shit they had come for – the fuel of their future – and was now explaining the quirks of the van. He said Nehemiah was lucky it wasn't a stick shift, since none of the kids knew how to drive a stick nowadays. He said Nehemiah should be careful anyways, though, since the gearshift didn't line up with the correct letters anymore. *Reverse means Park, Drive means Reverse. Etcetera, etcetera.*

On and on and on, like they weren't busting to get the hell out of there and be on their way. Repeating himself was the only glory Chicken Don had left. This is one-hundred percent what it means to be old, thought Nehemiah.

97

He was twenty-one himself and could drink every night if he wanted to. After leaving community college, borne away on an undertow of disgusted boredom, he had bounced around between his older brothers' various places, when their wives or girlfriends allowed it, sleeping on couches in living rooms or on futons in basements, minding his baby nieces and nephews for extra cash. So he had responsibilities, and also he didn't like alcohol. He didn't care to get drunk. He didn't like to feel out of control, and secretly he hated the taste of it, all of it, from the best craft beer down to the fumes of whatever depressing, nostril-burning gut rot was keeping Chicken Don alive.

Nehemiah smoked weed for hope, or to keep his anxiety down, and he took the occasional Xanny bar if the situation warranted, but he wasn't in thrall to them like Esmé. *Like almost every fucking person I know*, he amended, so he wouldn't be tempted to blame only her. "Everyone" meant his small clutch of friends, none of whom he was particularly pleased with anymore. None of whom he couldn't easily leave behind.

Leaving his family was harder. In certain moments, Nehemiah luxuriated in the truth: he was still the favorite. One of his older sisters, a talented sculptor almost making it in the city, had wired him the money to buy Chicken Don's van. No questions, no lectures. He knew they all worried about him, when they could, in between the chronic dramas of their own lives.

The closer he and Esmé got to the crazy sun and the Spanish moss and the ocean, that paradise – wasn't it bright and clear, like chlorine but more exciting? – the less burdened he would feel. In a month he'd be sending his siblings splashy updates in a group text: *Greetings from the seaside. Wish you were here. Srsly I love everyone to death.*

He would leave Dad out of it. Dad had gotten remarried and moved way downstate, and they almost never heard from him again. He was still kind, when you spoke to him – the same wandery-brained Dad, aloof and resigned. But he never got in touch first. He acted like having five kids had been some kind of car accident and now he was glad to leave the broken parts of that misfortune strewn down the road, turning the bend out of sight.

Esmé hated it all, too. She hated living in Bumfuck Lake Unincorporated, as she called their industrial hometown (the lake was polluted); hated grubby snow half the year and the only choices being big corporate agriculture or small hobby agriculture or the somehow-still-going, smoke-churning factory that could suck you in backwards for life, were you to drop your vigilance; hated the MAGA cretins, young and old – "cretin" was one of her favorite words. Her grades weren't good enough for her favorite university, the one with the big journalism school, and she didn't want to settle for the small state college where her puny scholarship was waiting for her.

But she didn't want to live at home anymore, either. That's how she went on, listing the dead ends in a raspy loop. Like a little song for him.

Given the chance to argue, she vibrated higher and higher. For instance, she didn't assume, like he did, that Chicken Don had purchased his wife from a foreign country. She had informed Nehemiah he was a racist and a misogynist for taking this viewpoint. *She's a person, not a conspiracy theory. Maybe she doesn't speak because she happens to be shy.*

But in another mood, she decided Chicken Don's wife had definitely been forced to marry him. She intended one day to investigate the matter and help the woman escape.

When it came to their own escape, though, the passion was in the planning of it, and Esmé had left all that to him. Of course she had. Her smothered only-child life, up till now – educated parents who had only her best interests in mind; who believed themselves saddened by their daughter's academic performance, which had proved only modest; who didn't get that Esmé's dramatic melancholy was the same as her optimism; who never left her alone for one minute so she could figure out how bad or good she truly wanted to be. It wasn't a mystery that she couldn't think for herself.

Nehemiah was scared Esmé loved his unconventional childhood more than she loved him. Him for him for him. It started with his hippie parents, exiling themselves ages ago from an Old Testament-flavored sect, using the pioneer-type skills they'd carried out of that life to build a house inside an old barn. Dad was a carpenter, whistling and brawny then, jazz loving and still spouting mild Scripture. Mom had homeschooled them, actually homeschooled them before it was any kind of a thing to do. Mom had made bread (bread that was often dinner, only the bread, no joke) and she made too many babies, as well (even now, wise as he'd grown, he thought of that as her doing) – until finally Dad had killed off the dream, went to work as a flagger for the NYSDOT, got himself a trickle of income to feed all their raggedy little mouths.

Nehemiah was hungry and handsome, but he had always hated his teeth. *My bedroom was inside a big horse stall when I was a kid*, he'd told Esmé when they first met. It had had an upright piano and a mattress in it. A horse blanket to keep warm.

Dude, it sounds like a cult. I mean your family itself, even after they left the actual cult. Just another cult, I tell you. She was a billion kinds of cute, with that snappy mouth and that pink hair cut up in shards like a Manga girl.

She seemed frail, sometimes, and that was the actual mystery. She had never had to search for anything to eat, not that he could tell. He envisioned a tiny girl-child at the end of a big table, her house with only three people in it where the scheme must have been food without end.

It was, indeed, a cult, he had replied. Sometimes he was terrified he lived just to please her.

They were going to stay with his thirty-three-year-old cousin, Wing, who lived just ahead of or just behind the Florida state line. Wing's wife had recently left him and so he was staying alone on a piece of his family's land. *That means it's your family land, too,* he'd messaged Nehemiah. *Technically speaking, of course.*

They had never met in person. Wing's aunt was one of Nehemiah's grandmothers, the one on his mother's side. *So we're first cousins*, Wing had rambled on, *but once removed.* Impossible. The kind of thing only a man with too much time on his hands could figure out.

Wing lived on the family land and plied his hushed trade; Nehemiah would help him with the shit he was bringing down from Chicken Don. At Wing's place, they could park Zelda until they got on their feet, pick up some straight jobs eventually, build a tiny house with what he could summon of Dad's carpentry skills. Ride down the road with live oaks to the beach every chance they got. Begin their life for real.

Once Esmé was eighteen, freedom would become their own invention. It wasn't that her parents didn't know about him. In fact, he knew all that was said of him because she had told him herself, brilliantly mocking their concerned understanding. *Interesting kid. Obviously bright. So much wasted potential.* His startled baby face, once his curse, was now his blessing – they believed her that he was seventeen, too, living under the guardianship of siblings and finishing up high school online. It was online that he'd found the Romeo & Juliet Law, which sided with statutory rapists in some states if the partners were close in age. Or so he thought he understood, until Wing had told him, *Doesn't fly unless you're both under eighteen, Dawg.* And he might be right.

Once Esmé's parents learned that he was really twenty-one, that he had taken their daughter away – during her senior-year spring break, no less, a month short of graduation – then the tune would rev up. Her parents seemed compassionate, or at least open-minded, but they were still her parents. No adults controlled his own life, so he couldn't trust any decision they would put in action.

• • •

When they finally pulled into Wing's yard, they had already been seeing palm trees for hours in the sticky twilight and Esmé was wide awake again, eating a miniature pecan pie from a roadside stop that had charmed them both with its random name: Pecan World.

Wing welcomed the fugitives with a rush of old-fashioned manners, gushing about the hell of a sixteen-hour drive, and how relieved they must be to be done with it. The house was the shape of a shoebox and made of cement, and the land stretched back like an open hand toward the sunset, the half-acre of yard a mix of sand and a few impressive architectural mounds erected by red ants. The grass was sparse and scrubby, but where it had color, it was emerald like a rainforest.

In the final measure of that long, long day, they found themselves sitting at a picnic table on Wing's back deck, shocked into a torpor by the screaming cicadas and eating delicatessen potato salad and charred hamburgers close to midnight. "Hope she's not a vegetarian," Wing said. He was a person who winked.

Nehemiah ducked his head. He was furious to be so embarrassed. He felt himself bare his teeth. He had an emotional-looking underbite – he had the same basic jaw as Wing. His cousin had come off sharper in his messages, quick thinking and practical. But the way he was carrying on now about his property, bragging about what-all he had in the world, when really it was so little, he was no more than a younger, less pickled version of Chicken Don.

"Happy to be eating finally," was all he said back.

Before they left on their journey, he'd assured Wing that the two of them would be content to sleep in Zelda. She was cozier than she looked, all rigged up with quilts and sleeping bags. But now he was hoping Wing would ask them inside for the night. Nehemiah had gone inside to piss and sussed out two small bedrooms at either end of the rectangle, hot in the shadows. Since it was only Wing and a couple of dogs living there, he figured one of those rooms had to be free.

"What's that awesome smell?" said Esmé. A wave of drastic delicate perfume was washing out of the dark.

"That's a bunch of Confederate Jasmine my Aunt Margie planted back in the day," Wing said. He gestured at a fortress of vine behind them that was devouring a rusty outbuilding. He said *Awnt*. "Aunt Margie was Nehemiah's grandmother, as he has probably told you. May she rest in peace." He was sucking on a long-necked beer bottle, getting juicy with authority.

Esmé stopped chewing. "*Confederate* Jasmine?" She raised one eyebrow at Nehemiah – she could do that. "Well, isn't that fucked up," she said to Wing.

Wing nodded. He was smiling. "You think it means something it doesn't."

"I mean," said Esmé, "don't think I wasn't checking the place for certain flags the minute we got here."

"Girl, you need an education." At least he said it lightly.

"Tell us what it means, then, Wing," said Nehemiah. He was slowly stabbing his knee with his fork, under the table.

"It's an Oriental plant," said Wing. "Invasive. AKA Star Jasmine. It comes from Malaysia." He paused to give their ignorance more suspense. "Formerly the Federation of Malaya. Hence the name."

Nehemiah laughed a little – not enough to hurt any feelings. "Sure," he said. "Because that's crystal clear. Why don't you just call it Star Jasmine?"

"Did you say *Oriental*?" Esmé drawled the last word.

"Yes ma'am, I did," said Wing.

She began rubbing her eyes. It was time for Nehemiah to see that she got to bed.

In the morning, they would explore, find the road he remembered, the live oaks ancient and weirdly liberated, even smothered under the Spanish moss, go out to the beach and swim under that good-god-what-sun till they were mute with joy, nothing but skin animals buoyed by salt. Maybe they would fuck underwater, for the novelty of it.

Make sure your pull-out game is strong, one of his older brothers had warned him – years ago now. And so far, it had been. He wouldn't try to finish in that manifesto of water, anyway. Just a little rhythm to establish their duet.

In the morning, however, she had so much to tell him. There was no time at all for him to lay out his scheme. He woke up in a state of profound depletion, thirsty and confused and cramped on Wing's saggy couch, a scuffed white controller boring into the small of his back.

"You passed out cold and I had no room," said Esmé, sitting on Nehemiah's chest wearing one of his T-shirts paired with her pastel Pusheen pajama bottoms. "I had to stay up talking to him. He gave me the spare bedroom. But don't worry, he left me alone."

"Where is he?" said Nehemiah. He could hear the wet hiss of a window air conditioner, but his entire body was already baptized in sweat. He wondered how far back in the van he was willing to dig to find a pair of shorts.

"Out back with the dogs," said Esmé. He sighed, drew her down to his chest and let her talk deep in his eardrum, that rasp rising and falling, a buggy little lament.

Wing was going out of town today, she told him. He was driving south, or maybe west. He was going to a protest about a Confederate general somewhere over in the Panhandle, he had said.

And it was even worse than it sounded. It was worse than Wing just being a random racist, she revealed. He was going to the protest because the Confederate general in question was his own great-great uncle. Or maybe it was his great-great-great uncle, this slave-owning bastard whose statue was being removed from the grounds of a college library, she explained.

It wasn't a college she had ever heard of. But it was true. He had shown her these documents, a family tree or some shit, confirming the relationship. Wing thought it was wrong to destroy history, especially his own history, she reported.

From where he lay, lazily smelling her, the situation was absurd. She sounded like a parent, like she was the mother and he, Nehemiah, was the father, and she was mocking their child's stupid behavior. She sat up again, still sitting on him, and he watched her like a movie. Her extravagant hand gestures were waking him up everywhere.

"I told him I thought the whole thing was unbelievably fucked," Esmé went on. Was she enjoying it, though? He thought she was, and more than a little bit, in fact. "Hey," Nehemiah lied. "I had no idea he was into this shit. Let him do his thing. It has nothing to do with us."

"You know what this means, right?" She came back to him. She folded her body with zero effort into half of its length – the most adorable poisonous toad in the entire world. She bit at his earlobes, pressed her little pelvis onto every inch of his morning erection. Even her breath smelled sweet this time of day. He inhaled canned corn.

"We're just here for safety," he said. Repeated. His voice was haggard; he was hearing the phrase as familiar music. "If you hate it we'll find a hotel the second you turn eighteen." He lifted his finger to indicate one week. He needed to sneeze, but the situation was serious. The carpet reeked of unwashed dog.

"It means you're related to a Confederate general too, you cretin." She was looking at his mouth like she might spit in it. He was relieved that her eyes were clear.

But the next shock was, Esmé didn't care to go searching for the beach with him. She was spending the day with Wing, instead, riding with him in his new truck. She was actually going to the protest with his cousin.

"It's better if we're not seen together for another week anyway," she said, and he had to nod: this was true.

It wasn't like she was attracted to Wing, she whispered, making this little fist. *Fucking hick!* Old enough to be her father if it had been a teen pregnancy, which was quite common around here, she was sure.

"About as common as in Bumfuck Lake Unincorporated," said Nehemiah.

But he knew she didn't want to hear about her own hypocrisy. She wanted action. Unlike Nehemiah, who remembered that beach so well, it was her first time in the South, she reminded him. He had made all the plans up till now, she complained. She wanted to take photos and get some quotes from the protesters on both sides, document an important historical moment. That was all.

He told her she would endanger herself there with all those leftist buttons pinned to her jacket. She would be a target; she might be identified as a runaway. She told him it was too hot for a jacket, anyway, and she wouldn't be wearing it.

She had to know what she was getting into, she added. Living in Georgia-Florida. Wherever the fuck they were now.

"I have to know for the sake of our future," she said, like a parent.

So he let them drive off, and then he got inside Zelda and shoved her into gear – *Neutral means Drive* – tearing down the sandy roads as hard as his fear of discovery would let him. A day spent pursuing some wild-ass notion of justice wasn't the same as abandonment – it was just Esmé being Esmé being Esmé – so of course she'd be back, and full of sulky guilt, too.

She'd been way too sheltered, and that was most of the problem. She was disoriented, she was coming down, she needed more, she was far from home. She was still only seventeen.

And he, Nehemiah, was the real child in the situation, he told himself, in the interest of fairness. He was the child for having expected a ride with no bumps.

He rolled down the grimy window and gasped for fresh news. No air conditioning in this evil van. And if there were live oaks anywhere on this road, they had either been cut down or were keeping out of his sightline. He screamed her name, paired it with the words "dumb" and "slut," through a lava slide of tears it took him a minute to register. His morning smoke had done nothing for the pain. A Xanny bar helped. Two would help more.

He didn't need a girlfriend, if you came right down to the very point. What he needed, what he had always needed, was a fucking time machine. The beach wasn't just further away than his own brand of memory – that vivid, picture-making gearwheel that was too close to dreaming – it was further away than the capability of his phone, too. No signal for the GPS. Only another betrayal.

And then, when he finally found it, the piece of ocean he remembered, it was closed due to excessive bacteria levels, and no one was around to explain to him what that actually meant. The foul message was decreed on a marching series of signs, all down this lonely road where the sugary dunes were netted off.

Somewhere behind a sagging pier he parked Zelda, who was finally overheating. The blue water was out there somewhere, all those curls of foam, bright-white lips – but shut off like this, it was as far away from him as it ever was.

After a while, he drove on. The next beach was private access only, and he almost went for it anyway – but he was calmer now, and wouldn't risk the attention. Instead he stopped at a convenience store, a sad-ass place from another decade with a pink flyer on the door announcing upcoming Easter services at a local church. Holiness right around the corner.

Trying not to sound desperate, trying not to sound too much like a Yankee to the weathered old woman behind the counter, he commenced a line of questioning. Urgent but polite. Slightly faster than slow.

"Oh hi, hey, how're you doing? *Ma'am*. So I'm looking for the closest beach you might have open today? I am definitely lost. Ha, ha."

If he glanced too high he could see the bird's-eye view of his body in the store's security mirror – greasy hair, humiliated shoulders, clothes gone soft with grime, long legs out of sight, red high-tops far at the bottom. Without his face to consider, he could be anyone at all. Without his face, anyone could score this whole journey any way they saw it.

The words he'd been shoving away for weeks crashed over him. *Statutory Rape. Sex offender. Wanted in two states.*

More than two, actually. If you counted all the states they'd driven through just to get here, it could play out forever.

Blight + Cotillion

Maggie was in charge of her much younger half sister for the rest of June. It was already pretty hot out, for the mountains. The little girl's bed was a mildewed camping cot they set up by the woodstove for her, covered with quilts, a Snoopy sleeping bag, and an old pillow the little girl had brought from home. In the morning she ate her breakfast in a flinching way, watched for the cabin's tiny bathroom to be empty, then sped in there and stayed way too long while Maggie and Jamie locked eyes about the situation. Gently, they kicked at one another's ankles under the table in the cabin's small main room. A map of the constellations was tacked to the ceiling above them.

The table was small, too; Jamie had carved it for them out of this rare wormy-chestnut wood he'd traded for. The two seats were made from a different, more common wood. He'd shaped them long and backless, like pews or benches. Barley, their elderly brown mutt, was usually lodged under one of them, wheezing.

Corinne came out of the bathroom with red eyes. She looked neither right nor left.

Maggie encouraged her to come back to the table and finish her cereal. She thought eight was too young for a child to look so tired, but she was impressed by the girl's clear disgust. Maggie had learned long ago to keep her own expression smooth. Now that was what everyone liked her for, and it was all too late. A friend in college had compared Maggie to the Mona Lisa, and that seemed flattering enough to shape her life around. Corinne had the same high, helpless forehead. A pleat had formed between her eyebrows – she wasn't even in third grade.

That was blood, Maggie reasoned, although the father they shared – an over-articulating old lawyer who had enjoyed keeping them apart – wasn't really the connection. It might even have something to do with their mothers, who had never met. Both of them, a generation apart, had been his legal secretaries-turned-lovers, their liberty wrecked by that mad, charming man. Maggie didn't want to admit the pattern; in her mind, both of these women had been tricked into marrying Dad, and desire didn't have a say.

Anyway, her own mother still refused to bring it up, and Corinne's mother had only recently gotten free. That's why the child had been sent to Maggie's: they needed her out of the way until the shock settled, or until her mother found her own apartment.

Since Corinne wouldn't talk much about the separation or anything else, Maggie had to plan the days. In the time they had, she figured she could show Corinne how to sew or learn contra dancing – something only Maggie could teach her.

By then Maggie was twenty-six. Only a few weeks before, she had finished her degree in folklore in the department of American Studies. Her head was full of old-time ballads, memorized *a cappella*: the lovely creeping cadence, the minor modes. Her voice was light and reedy, not important. They were ancient ballads from Scotland and Ireland, carried over to the Southern mountains. The theme was usually some big passion that led to murder – but also murder for the mere sake of it, a blown-up storm. The ballads were about fond notions brought down.

These were only the first days! Already the visit felt long. At night, after Jamie got home from his landscaping job and they made dinner together and ate it together at their homemade table, he went to his tiny workspace, an addition off the back of the cabin they rented.

The addition was only half a room. It had a severely slanted roof, and a smallish man like Jamie couldn't stand up in it all the way. But there was a window in it that looked right up the mountain, and he could sit on a stool and tend to what was in front of him: a model of a battlefield, with dozens of miniature soldiers he had molded of clay and baked in the big industrial kiln, back on campus. Jamie had taken his own degree in pottery.

He and Maggie, they had been at that little college so long that even now, as graduates, they couldn't climb out of the culture.

They still went to the weekly dance, held in the hundred-year-old barn behind the Fine Arts building. There was a newer, lower barn that sat in the valley, built for students who were cutting their tuition doing farm work-study. Jamie and Maggie had worked on the farm, learning homesteading skills, although it wasn't enough money to keep her in school, not after so many years. They both tried to learn to play, he on the banjo, she on the fiddle, but the talent wasn't there, far less the discipline, and they decided they weren't musicians, but rather enjoyers. She began borrowing money.

With Jamie deep in history and the sunset coming on, the sisters went out back to the garden patch. The yard was a fourth acre that dipped out of sight at the perimeter, heading down toward a small creek. Beyond that was a trail that turned into national-forest land.

The trailhead was hidden by waxy, dark-green heath – the kind of thicket the settlers called "hells." Once upon a time, the hells were so thick people would actually get lost in them. And die.

It was true. Jamie was proud to tell Corinne about the hells, early on, but he stopped his flow of information – his hands in the air – when he saw how the girl looked at him. She watched him like a movie clown: a made-up demon who told silly stories.

Close up, the few blooms of mountain laurel left on the heath bushes looked like miniature teacups out of an old-fashioned dollhouse. Viewed through a far squint, they looked like pieces of litter.

Maggie could feel Corinne eyeing her flowered dress. It was a thrift-store find. Maggie had let out the tight darts in the torso to make room for her significant, sloped breasts; she'd enhanced the skirt with wide work pockets, sewn on from the remnants of a different dress, with a different but similar flowered print. Maggie's long hair went down in a plain low braid pointed at her lower back, but her little sister wore a short wedge style, cut at a salon.

They'd already picked the season's first lettuce for their dinner, the last few nights, and a mess of radishes. Corinne had removed the sliced radishes from her salad, making a delicate project of lining them up in a fan pattern on her spatterware plate.

Now Maggie bent over to thin out the snap beans that were starting to flower and run toward each other. "Help me separate these?" she said, and showed Corinne how to bury her hands among the runners.

Their quiet competed with the crickets – that warm, rising appeal. Maggie paused to rub the back of her wrist against her mouth.

"I'm going to have to get an actual job sooner or later," she said, studying her beans. An earthy breeze was blowing a protest through the garden. "My student loans come due this fall. But I'm putting it off as long as I can."

"Oh," said Corinne. She looked like a foal, kneeling in the dirt with her skinny legs folded out to the side. When her older sister turned away, Corinne took her hands out of the beans and just sat there.

Maggie sniffed; she wasn't finished. "So anyway, it's nice that I can be with you this summer," she said. "If I had to work, you couldn't have stayed here." She fingered a pale bean flower.

"Is this what you call 'back to the land?'" Corinne said. The dry voice coming out of that child was a shock.

"Is 'back to the land' what Dad calls it?" That would be like him, making fun of his older daughter and her boyfriend. Having a ball with their lifestyle. He would say "lazy" or "hippies" or both. He would hint that they were losers, or at least not moving forward in the right way – as though what they loved, everything about the life she and Jamie were making together, wasn't really their choice but just a crazy mistake: a skidmark on a country road, going into a ditch.

At the same time, she had been away from him long enough to realize how far he could go with this game, playing around with both sides. In his letters to Maggie, he had called his own handsome home "blighted" and "soulless." He had a big house on the edge of the city, that he had shared, until recently, with Corinne and her mother. It was new; it had new, fake columns. He was disgusted with Yuppies – he composed spectacular, bitter sentences about them the same way he had, not that long ago, written about Reagan. Maggie remembered his favorite phrase: "that washed-up actor in the White House."

He had once read *Walden Pond* in its entirety, her father reminded Maggie. Inspired by this memory, he revealed he had also written a well-received essay about the Transcendentalists, during his years at the university – the one he had wanted her to go to.

He declared this and that; he took up every inch. He said he *truly admired* how she and Jamie were shunning the *materialistic excesses* of their decade – his handwriting was calligraphy – and getting back in touch with what was real. It was a perfect time for the two sisters to get to know each other, he wrote, and he was *utterly pleased at the timeliness of the endeavor, given the unfortunate turn of events regarding the child's mother.* He asked Maggie how her own mother was doing.

But Maggie's mother was out west in Santa Fe, living in the supply room of a coffeeshop with a boyfriend of her own, the man who ran the place and lived there too. It seemed New Mexico was getting expensive. She sent a photo: The coffeeshop was made of adobe with a screaming turquoise door. The sun looked festive, really unstoppable.

Her mother approved of Maggie's lifestyle. But Maggie wished she'd quit bugging her to come visit, because she never asked her to bring Jamie to New Mexico, too. Like she was jealous of him, being so much a part of her. Her parents – they both wanted her back, now, though when she was growing up, they had hardly noticed her.

She resented her mother and father like the fat towers of rainclouds that nosed over the mountain on the afternoons she decided to work in the sun, piecing out a quilt she was making from old sweatshirts.

"He definitely said 'back to the land,'" said Corinne.

"You can call it that if you want to," said Maggie. "We like to live the way people used to, out here." She rattled over her lines.

"It feels more authentic to make things with our hands instead of buying everything. We want a simple life."

Once they had their own cabin, instead of just renting one, Jamie wanted to build an outhouse. If they accepted a piece of land without running water, they could be homeowners that much sooner. They could have their own chickens, and thus their own eggs, instead of getting eggs at the co-op. Jamie knew she wanted a flock of hens. In Maggie's imagination, they were already named, each one after a tragic girl in one of the old ballads: Pretty Saro and Pretty Polly. Young Emily, Peggy-O. *Little Maggie.*

Except she couldn't name a chicken after herself. That was going too far. Her parents had christened her Margaret Elizabeth, after her two grandmothers. They still called her Beth; she'd been a Beth for her first twenty years, and they couldn't change for her.

Suddenly she wanted to apologize to her little sister for not having cable television. "I'll take you to the library soon," she said, both of them standing there in the fading boil of twilight. "I was really into the *Little House* books when I was your age. In a way I never grew out of it." She had been waiting to say this. Now it made her blush.

She said, "I know you must miss your friends. I know about going through a divorce. It's the worst."

Corinne rolled her eyes. Then her eyes began filling up. She didn't look like she wanted a hug. Maggie could see Jamie's head through the grimy window of his workshop. She would begin crying herself, soon, and all she wanted was to be alone with her lover, in the proud, cracked, old iron bed they had picked out together. His hands would roam tentatively over her body, wondering and wondering about all this fuss.

The next day they had a sewing lesson, but Maggie could tell it was futile. Corinne let her sister thread the needle for her, not accepting the challenge to locate the little eye herself. She worked the piece of cotton Maggie gave her for forty-five minutes while she twisted and untwisted her legs around a table leg. Then she put her sewing aside and went out to the tire swing that Jamie had hung in the double-trunk basswood tree in the front yard.

From there, the view was a country highway. The long blue hills brewed in their layers. The quiet was even quieter in between the retreat and advance of long-haul trucks. In their dream cabin, they wouldn't hear the road at all.

Maggie let Corinne do her own thing. They would go out tonight, to the Friday night dance at the old barn. Things might be getting better. That morning, her sister had gone into the bathroom and spent only a few minutes.

When she came back, she had something in her hand. It was a homemade washcloth with several holes torn in it, like a piece of Swiss cheese. Maggie had made it and others like it from an old beach towel, stitching the four sides with rows of little red Xs, for a pretty contrast.

Corinne sat down at the table, where Jamie was still eating his scrambled eggs. She accepted a glass of orange juice from her sister. She even set her feet on the round back of Barley, who was napping under the bench, and massaged his stinky coat with her toes. The dog thumped his tail on the wooden floor.

"He likes that," said Maggie. Corinne was smiling a little. She smoothed the ragged square with her fingers.

"You know what?" she said. "This is one sad, sad washcloth."

Maggie hadn't heard Jamie laugh so loud in a long time – like her, he was worried about money.

When the sun got hot mid-afternoon, she led her sister over the creek, up to the trailhead out back. They ducked through all the heath, scratched their arms, and walked along the old forest-service road for a mile. They were heading to a swimming hole. Gnats bothered them a little, but nothing else. Maggie pointed out flame azaleas and the last of the spiky firepinks.

In the trees it was lush. The odor was heavy, full of seed and sweet, breeding rot.

The rhododendrons at this elevation were almost over. Higher up, Maggie knew, they would still be blooming. But if they followed the trail up too many miles, the way she would have done with Jamie, the water there would be too cold for a child from the city. Even so, when she forked left at the first big clearing – there was a deep pool there, shaped by boulders; it threw truth like a mirror into the shushing small river – she figured the water was no more than sixty degrees.

"Think of describing this to your friends," she told Corinne. Maggie wore her old string bikini with a tie-dyed T-shirt over it, a contra-dance shirt from years ago, designed by one of the more energetic students who thought she could formalize the scene with shirts and other souvenirs, ordering memento after memento from the print shop. She had made up titles for the dances, every semester, but none stuck. The T-shirt showed one of these titles, written in lacy script – "High Country Cotillion." The logo was a dancing couple in silhouette. On the back was the name of their college and the year.

She explained contra dancing to Corinne as they sat on a boulder with their feet in the shocking water. "Dad makes jokes about it being the Iran Contras," she said.

"I know," said Corinne.

"But it has nothing to do with that," said Maggie. She said it was old; she said it was innocent. She told her sister to imagine that "Contra" meant country.

"So, Dad said you were good at math. This dance is kind of mathematical. It goes in a pattern, and it's so fun once you get the hang of it."

"Okay," said Corinne.

"Now it's just called the Friday Night Dance or the Barn Dance. It's not called High Country Cotillion anymore. No one expects you to learn the steps right away."

"Okay," said Corinne.

"But we love it. We've been doing it forever."

Sometimes Maggie took hers and Jamie's soiled clothing down to the creek with an old tin washboard they had found at an antique store, and did their laundry that way, with a bottle of liquid peppermint soap from the co-op. She always wanted to give more and more of herself to the cold water. She had a method: she crouched on the big rock, rocking back on her heels, and meditated a few minutes to gather some heat – then jumped suddenly, going in all the way. A little shout was all it took to recover from the pain.

Now Corinne was above her, still sitting on the rock, looking down. Maggie paddled on her back and kept her face turned toward her sister. Poplar trees mobbed up high above them, with the buttonwoods reaching out and down, bending to touch the water. The ridgetop was a sunny green at the height of the day, and only went blue, as was promised, when the sun was coming up or going down.

The crazy-cold immersion was a revelation – it still was, after so many years. "Dad wanted me to be a lawyer, like him," said Maggie. "And obviously I'm not doing that." She dipped her head back until her hair had disappeared in the water and only her face was showing. "But I want you to know something. You don't actually have to do anything he wants you to do. You don't have to do what he says, when you grow up and get out of there. Eventually he won't be able to do anything about who you are."

Before the dance that night, Maggie unbraided her long, damp hair and put on a blouse with an embroidered yoke chest and her favorite circle skirt and black cloth sandals with roses printed across the toes, sold at the co-op during the warmer months. She was pretty; she was even strong. They drove to campus in the old truck. Jamie wore something clean and put on his cowrie necklace.

They found their friends and sat around outside the old barn, where log stumps were placed in opposite rows for seats. Jamie rolled a cigarette from his pouch of American Spirit tobacco and Maggie butted her head against his shoulder. She took in warm cloth, and warm body, and the Appalachian summer that would always advance just this way, smug with four hundred million years of practice.

Maggie was dreading the first dance a little. She wasn't a student anymore; she didn't want to look like she thought she was. But having Corinne with them was new.

They went inside and saw Steve and Donna, whose wedding they had attended that spring, in the old stone chapel on campus; and big, handsome Brian and his girlfriend Shelby, who was just twenty-one. No alcohol could be served at the contra dances, but of course Brian had already been drinking. They lived in a dry county here, but ten miles away, in the next town, was a convenience store that sold cheap beer.

They smelled liquor on him, actually. He knew where some of the original families were still making moonshine, in certain hollers, and so did Abraham, one of the oldest dancers. He taught at the college, and was closer to their parents' age.

Abraham had taken on a leadership role, lately, filling in the need for order. Someone had to keep the barn open for Friday nights. Someone had to select the bands. "This is my little sister," Maggie said.

Corinne still wore her tank top and shorts. "Wonderful," said Abraham, leaning down in a courtly way. Everything about him snaked out of that long, graying beard. "Will she be dancing with us tonight?" he asked, irritably.

"Probably just watching," said Maggie. Abraham walked over to the stage to discuss the night's repertoire, his hand on his hip where Wrangler jeans were held up by a braided narrow belt.

After the fiddler, a bony woman from New England, called the figures and broke into song, Jamie and Maggie joined the long lines of dancers, and the pleasure of ritualized movement exerted its familiar triumph. Her anxiety stepped out.

Corinne sat cross-legged on one of the haystacks scattered around the wide-planked barn floor. Already the air was humid from so many humans.

The actives fluidly rotated their partners down the line and fell into eye contact, as tradition demanded. The others, the ones waiting to dance, laughed at their own and others' false starts, and tried to resume the flow. A few dancers were new, rising sophomore girls in summer school; they'd arrived together in a bored little pack. Abraham was focused on one of them.

The summer-school student he liked couldn't be older than nineteen, Maggie thought. She was chatty and reckless. She had a banner of nice teeth. She was laughing harder than anyone else at the confusion of the beginners; she saw that this was terribly funny.

Maggie could never tell for sure what was merry and what was mocking. When she was Corinne's age, at school, she had giggled during the Pledge of Allegiance one morning. A friend had made her giggle; she couldn't remember why. And her teacher that year – hadn't she adored him, up till then? – he had screamed in her face. He exploded like a star. She was disrespectful! His own friends had come home in body bags, he said. Would she enjoy Vietnam?

They were half an hour in, heaving lightly. The music rose and rose, but when the line of actives joined in a flourish, linking pinkies for the collective turn, the air abruptly went wrong. It came down.

When the summer-school student fell to her knees, Maggie dropped out of Jamie's arms, even though they were the head couple, and felt the head couple's burden of duty. She didn't go to the source of the scream; she went to find Corinne. The band was still playing – it sounded like a Cape Breton tune, not her favorite. The fiddler sawed on. Up there, on the wooden stage, the band didn't realize yet there had been an incident.

It unfolded that Abraham had held on to the summer-school student's pinkie too long, trying to slow her turn. It was a mistake, he said. His voice had lost its control. He had managed to hurt the student's little finger. It seemed he had actually broken it.

They left then – it wasn't even intermission. Maggie made the decision. In the truck, she pulled Corinne onto her lap and Jamie took the curves home. It was mountain-dark. Two scenes battled in Maggie's head: one was the disgrace of the summer-school student, all hot and hurt in a mess on the ground, grieving her finger. The other was her little sister's unexpected journey. When the pinkie broke, Corinne had run into the stopped line of dancers, meeting Maggie exactly where Maggie went to find her. She let her older sister grip at her, look into her face, and lead her out.

"I don't want you to think it's usually like that," she said, once they were home. She said it more than once. Her body was still overheated.

"It was fun until that happened," said Corinne. They laughed for a long time. Then she said, "I liked going to the swimming hole today." They were really together, suddenly, in the little cabin. "Abraham is kind of a jerk, to be totally honest," Jamie said, rubbing out his last American Spirit for the night against the open doorjamb. "Even if he didn't mean to hurt her, there's still no excuse. He needs to chill the heck out."

He spoke some low words to Barley; all week, he'd been trying to coax the dog to sleep next to Corinne on her cot. They said goodnight to the little girl and went to their room.

Maggie closed the door quietly and took off her clothes. Underneath her shirt and skirt, she wore an old silk camisole, likely from the 1940s, and plain cotton underwear. She opened the bedroom window for air and stayed there, staring into darkness over her folded arms, until she figured her sister was asleep. Then she got into their iron bed, under their flowered sheets and faded army blanket, and took off everything else.

"That old mother*fucker*," said Jamie, who was naked. "I wonder what happens now."

"I know, I know," Maggie whispered. She was still hearing fiddle tunes, smelling woodsmoke and mold. She put her arms around this kind, strong man, and drew his hands down, placed his fingers on her body exactly where she wanted them to be. She gripped her legs around his waist, like a man's murderous hands around a faithless lover's neck in one of the great old songs, until he knew how hard she meant it, and demanded he give her a baby.

The Miracle of Flight

"That won't hurt you, it's a kind of plane," Caroline said. Misty whipped her head up to follow the noise. A roar that was obviously hell's lawnmower destroyed the air just above them, but just as fast the sky was empty again. A finger of smoke probed the tree line.

Lance inside his Ultralight was in control. The older son of the Sluders, he tilted his aircraft behind the warm bulge of oaks that separated his family's farm, with its vast scroll of cabbages running back to the horizon and its summer farm stand, Sluder Family Produce, facing the country highway – this continual invitation – from the half acre where Caroline lived, with her parents, in a little white house with a side garden. Their old hand-cranked well was painted glistening red, but they never used it.

They turned back to the tire swing, bored again. Misty was thirteen, two years older than Caroline but only a grade ahead. When school started next week, she would be in seventh grade instead of eighth. Caroline would enter sixth.

Misty had been left back a year, a long time ago. She had a little waistline, little breasts, and a gap between her front teeth. Those teeth rested lightly against Misty's full bottom lip when she smiled, but the flaw was nothing more than a crack in a porcelain teacup.

Misty went to school in the city, where life was apparently rough or glamorous. She only rode out here every other weekend in the summer, to visit her lonely grandparents. The grandparents lived in a candy-pink house across the road and weren't that much older than Caroline's own parents, who had started late.

Those were Misty's words. "Your parents are how old? They must have started late."

Caroline turned away. She reached down to her heel, exposed by a rubber flip-flop, and stripped off a piece of dead skin. She put it secretly in her mouth. She was just an American girl living in the country, but she had recently stolen an accent she imagined to be from the moors. "I imagine they did start a little late," Caroline said, and began to chew.

She was called an advanced reader. Her parents wouldn't visit Misty's chain-smoking grandparents in the candy-pink house and they also stayed away from the farming Sluders, whose life, that whole song and system, remained huge and distant. All summer Caroline had wondered whether fields crawled over by tractors could be considered moors.

Caroline looked forward to Misty just like she looked forward to the summer's forward march of berries, living lower than the trees or the cabbages, buggy and discoverable: blackberries, wineberries, and, right now, the sweet muscadine grapes. She glared secretly at Misty, who was tall and didn't think to stoop. Misty's voice was already a young woman's voice – she didn't even have to try.

Sometimes having this friend was a rising hope. But then Misty spoke, killed the hope like a plain hammer. "Most assuredly one of the commoners," whispered Caroline in her best accent.

When Misty's questions dribbled out of her, as mindless as an old dog banging its tail on a mudroom floor, Caroline wanted to rub the older girl's attractive face in the dirt. *Shut up. Shut up. You're having an attack.*

It was a phrase lifted dimly from adults. She was eleven, she had seen a few things: a barn cat drooling mad with daydreams, swaying side to side, having an attack of distemper.

She had been raised to view bad manners as the outcome of low intelligence. But if Misty's questions were smarter than she had dared imagine – if it was just the way of the city – then the attack was on her – Caroline.

"Have you started growing yet?" Misty asked. She smiled at the younger girl, the same smile she gave her dog. "No, dopey, I don't mean height ... stick out your chest. See mine?"

Misty asked: "If both your parents teach at a college, why aren't you a genius?"

She went on like this all summer.

"Do your parents like Carter or Reagan?"

"Why is your hair so short? Do you let your mother cut it or do you go to a place? Do you want to look like a boy?"

"Am I your only friend?"

Misty lisped a little; sometimes spit came out on that plump, carved-looking bottom lip, but it didn't kill her glory. She swished her long ponytail back and forth, getting rid of flies that weren't there. Caroline pulsed with the urge to imitate – but that was impossible. Instead, she quietly gouged her thumb cuticles until she could feel the breeze against fresh blood.

Now Misty sat in the middle of the tire swing and Caroline, with her wobbly mantis legs, balanced on top of it. They maneuvered the rope as a pair, banging themselves, safe inside the tire, deliberately against the tree, a red oak so big two girls couldn't hug their arms around it and hope to touch. From this position, they watched the advance of Lance's brother, Leif, who was only seven years old.

He was creeping across the woodsy, humid property line to be with them. "Why is he so much younger?" asked Misty. "Is he adopted? Is he a half brother?" Misty had a half brother herself, in the military. Caroline could only answer wisely that Lance and Leif not only had names that sounded alike, but they looked alike, too, and this was easy to see, forget about the age difference. She meant to ask her father what a half brother was.

Lance was out of their league, eighteen, not in high school but already seeming far beyond it. Last year he had dropped out. "Were his parents pissed off?" asked Misty. "Does he have to work for them all the time now?" He was even married, to his tiny girlfriend RaeAnn, who was seventeen. She had dropped out with him.

Caroline had a hard time not thinking about it. What could love do? It wasn't like cancer or insanity, a thing you couldn't help, that would bring sympathy. You did love to yourself, or at least, you didn't try to stop it. Did it have that much power, stamping out all other miseries? Could it be caught? Taught? Caroline dreamed about it lushly; then she would wake up worried.

She knew better than to ask about it out loud, though – here was her power. However it had happened, RaeAnn was Lance's wife now. She lived with him and was a Sluder, too, together with all of the Sluders in the same noisy Sluder house.

Misty wanted to know whether Lance and RaeAnn slept in the same bedroom Lance had had growing up or if they got to have another room, now. "How do they do it with everyone around? What if she gets knocked up? Or is she already knocked up? Is that why they got married?"

Caroline hummed through the attack, hummed and gnawed at her latest canker sore – wretched – till she could speak again. Leif had a special condition, she told Misty. "So you can't make fun of him," she said. "You can't confuse him with too many questions."

Talking low about that little boy was important. It made her heart thump. What he had, it didn't make him dangerous – she didn't believe that anymore, now that she was eleven – but it was better to be careful.

"Is he retarded?" asked Misty.

Caroline blushed. "He has a special condition," she said again. Leif thrashed through an opening in a stand of overgrown black walnut where the girls sometimes climbed high up to have a better look at the Sluder farm and see what Lance was doing, and, lately, to get a glimpse of RaeAnn.

They winced at the sight of the little boy so deep inside their lookout. But now he was beyond it and walking up to them, there on the swing, having gotten a long stick to pull behind him like a leash attached to no animal. His hair faded dirty into its own shadows, long enough to cover the ringed collar of his striped T-shirt.

"Hey, Leif," said Caroline, adjusting her glasses against her nose with the absolute tip of her pinky. She spoke kindly, to show Misty what education was.

He stared at them with his filmy blue eyes. "Lance and RaeAnn got in a fight last night," he said. "He went up in the Ultralight this morning. But Daddy needs him on the baler. Mama's going to get me Sea Monkeys for my birthday."

His special condition was in the way he didn't blink. Caroline was an only child, but she did have cousins, and the little ones especially were always too sodden with emotion, either crying about something they couldn't have or laughing at something not funny. They were boring – they screamed – they made a smart person want to hide.

Leif was different. His voice was like the metronome her mother set on the piano during Caroline's practice time. Tack, tack, tack.

"How about a pet rock?" asked Misty. "You know you can train it."

Leif nodded and slid his stick lovingly against the old oak. "You train em," he said. "Where do you get em?"

"At the Pet Rock Store," said Misty. They had both jumped off the swing and stood there facing the little boy, as though this could ever be important. "Just like you get Sea Monkeys at the Sea Monkey Store."

Caroline gave her a look. "You're going to get your Sea Monkeys out of the back of a comic book," she said gently. She wanted to change the subject forever. "So RaeAnn is your sister-in-law now. 'Sister-in-law' is a legal word."

They lived around that idea a minute. The Ultralight groaned in the clouds, an engorged mechanical wasp with landing gear trailing down. Caroline thought about Lance and RaeAnn wrapped around one another – alone in some hot room, in the dark, risking all of their dignity. How could they do that and then shuffle back into the day intact, face all of those painful lesser hours?

"It's bam!" said Leif. They jumped. "And then it's bam, bam." He began striking the tree trunk with his stick. "And then it's bam, bam, bam," he finished, whacking the tree three times.

His expression never varied – it aimed for perfection. Misty said, "Oh, *what?*" She bent over and put her hands over her mouth. Her shoulders began to shake, folding toward the front like wings.

"Tell us what you mean by that," said Caroline.

He shrugged a shoulder, studying a point on the ground. Caroline wondered where Leif's friends were, the little boys from school. He should be past kindergarten now; he would be in first or second grade. Why hadn't she seen him in the halls last year? Or had she? Their little beige-bricked school was so small, not like Misty's school in the city that sprawled over a half block, as big as some of the buildings at the university.

Before he married RaeAnn, Lance had had plenty of his own friends, she remembered, other teenage boys, deep voiced and menacing – like him. They made fires somewhere in the unreal vastness of the Sluder property. You could hear the thrill of their voices when the wind went just so.

She hadn't heard them this summer, though. Maybe you had to give up your old friends when you got married. Her parents didn't seem to have any, or anyway none that came out to the country.

"Lance and RaeAnn got in a fight last night," Leif said.

"You said that already," said Misty. She let one hand drop gracefully to her hip. "So what was the fight about?"

"He went up in the Ultralight today," said Leif.

"Sure enough." Misty looked at Caroline. "This is going nowhere." Her shrillness went up and down – but not as sure as the cicadas.

Caroline remembered then they were supposed to be picking grapes so her mother could make grape juice. "You can help us," she told Leif, "but you really have to try to do a good job, and you can't eat any." He turned obediently and walked toward the grape arbor, a bastille of green – leaves like desperate little hands – that grew behind her parents' vegetable garden.

The grapes flourished, but her parents were letting the garden die, in slow sections, since it was almost fall – they were nothing like the Sluders, who reaped things uncontrollably and would keep harvesting through the very end of October. Even now, the pumpkins in the fields were replacing the cabbages, a rash of orange starting to run up the back hill. In October, Caroline could pick out one free pumpkin, since she was a neighbor.

Leif seemed to decide about something, something against grapes. He gripped his stick and turned into the black-walnut stand, nosing again for his own property.

The girls turned around in the other direction, toward the house. At the same moment, they decided to run. They found two colanders and ran out again. The colanders were mismatched: one was rusty metal and the other was new and plastic. The kitchen had a potbellied woodstove and two doors, in the old style, one to the side yard and one out to the back.

They got themselves settled among the grapes, and there, after a quiet spell of sucking (you tore through the thick skin of the grape with your teeth and then spit it out to get to the seedy, ultrasweet center) and plunking the less desirable specimens into the colanders, they decoded Leif's language – his little fit – and translated what he had been trying to tell them. It was this: Lance was beating RaeAnn – he was going to kill her, that was the main thing – and it was their job to stop it.

. . .

Instead of going back to her grandparents' house after supper, Misty slept over. They dragged Caroline's saggy old bed mattress onto the floor for Misty. That left the naked box spring for Caroline, which she covered with a sleeping bag.

They talked late. They had barely eaten the corn on the cob (from Sluder Family Produce) and hot dogs Caroline's mother had set out on the porch for them. They had barely drunk the milk. They rattled their chipped china plates when they scraped them. They drained their glass tumblers into the old porcelain sink. It was important to hurry, because after dinner they had to look for clay to make a voodoo doll.

Caroline found it on a shelf in the craft room, where her mother kept her sewing machine and a shoebox overflowing with Simplicity and Butterick patterns and a pincushion like a fat tomato with a baby tomato hanging off it – the needle cleaner – plus the debris of unfinished projects in other materials: wires and clamps from an earring-making kit and this unused clay, just a pack of gray sticks. Caroline's mother liked to work with her hands in the summer, after teaching Freshman Composition all year to old teenagers, eighteen and nineteen, who didn't appreciate what she wanted from them: a succession of clear sentences supporting the main idea.

Her father was a professor of earth sciences. But this summer, with no classes to occupy him, he was caught up fast by the arrogance of the Ultralight. He said it was nothing more than a hang glider with a motor. He wondered who had allowed it.

"It's remarkable," he had muttered one morning, early June – drowning his big mustache inside his favorite pottery mug

– "it's remarkable that the miracle of flight is now accessible to an average uneducated teenager." It was an outrage: a real working aircraft, assembled from a kit. "What he's doing, essentially, is operating a man-sized model plane. A toy in the air. Inconceivable."

"The miracle of flight," Caroline had mocked, in a voice like her *Peter and the Wolf* record. Sometimes she was afraid she really loved her father the most. "*Inconceivable!*" she said. Her father frowned dramatically. He lectured. An Ultralight was controlled by the shifting weight of its pilot's legs; therefore the top speed wasn't even in the same league as a crop duster. Lance couldn't go any faster than a car might go: a car observing the posted speed limit.

Her mother said it was louder than a car with its muffler sawed off. "You'll be inclined to agree," she added.

But it was dark by now, probably ten o'clock. The boxspring felt like a punishment, so Caroline threw her sleeping bag down on the worn Turkish rug that covered the splintery floor. These rugs were all through the house, in slightly different patterns; in her bedroom, the soft panorama was roses blooming out of oysters.

It was cooler down there, away from the close, heavy eaves. "You're holding my real bed hostage," she complained to her friend, observing this girl – who was she again? – stretched out long-legged and comfortable on the stolen mattress.

It was a word Caroline had heard on the news. And seen, behind the gray-suited anchorman, night after night. *The Iranian hostage crisis. Today is Day 300.*

"Never mind. We have to work." Misty was shaping the voodoo doll. They knew about witchcraft from their secret book, hidden inside one of the milk crates they were using for seats in the walnut-tree lookout. Now, after months in the elements, its pages were stiff and spotted with mildew: *Olde Spells and the Art of Magick*. Misty had gotten it from the adult section of the library, back in the city.

She didn't intend to give the book back – she would ruin her library privileges over it. Sinister. *Olde Spells* had a black cover and in truth it was hard to get through, just too many pages of spidery diagrams that looked alike but were intended to move toward a goal, and stories with pen-and-ink portraits, mostly about old witches and old warlocks whose very deaths, long ago in other centuries, seemed to prove some failure of power.

But it bound them. Misty said she made love potions from the book, sometimes. It was possible she had a boyfriend waiting for her, back in the city. It was possible he was in ninth grade.

A voodoo doll, according to the book, was entirely foolproof. But first you had to retrieve something personal from the intended victim, a piece of clothing or a strand of hair, to mold into the figure.

Before that came the likeness. They stretched the clay to make the doll tall and skinny. They rolled two pieces carefully to form the legs and pinched in little sneaker shapes at the end of them. That part of the body seemed most important, since – Caroline now told Misty – Lance steered the Ultralight with his feet.

They used the head of one of the pins they had taken from the pincushion to prick in tiny features. Later they would stick

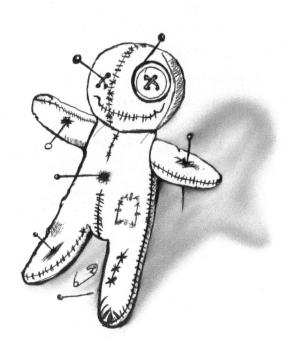

the doll all through with the pins from the pincushion and bury it somewhere on the Sluder property so that Lance would wreck the Ultralight and die, or at least be hurt and immobilized, and RaeAnn would be free.

Caroline gently fingered the top of the clay head to mold the hairstyle worn by the Sluder boys. Overgrown. Unrepentant.

They talked about RaeAnn, reverently prying her apart. Caroline remembered her from the school bus, number 691, where kindergarteners through seniors all rode together: their town was that small. RaeAnn was one of the older girls still stuck on there because she didn't have her own car yet. She was short as a child, but in jeans she had a figure – a breezy way about her – shy – not so shy. Caroline knew RaeAnn had her own horse at home: this was easily observed from the bus windows.

"One time," said Caroline, "my bus driver became furious." She got excited and dropped her British accent. "He stopped the bus because it was hailing, and we were being too loud and wrecking his concentration. Not me. But he said he'd throw us all out on the side of the road." She scratched under her nightgown. "I mean to die."

"That's mental," said Misty. "Did he leave you?"

"Naturally he did not," said Caroline. "But RaeAnn was on there and she was scared silly. It was like she thought he would hit her. She went back to the last seat. She hid under it." As she told it, it became real.

"Holy shit," said Misty. "*Bam!*"

"Don't wake up my parents," said Caroline. She showed her how to whisper: "Bam. Bam."

The next part, stealing a personal item from Lance's body –
it would be like trying to budge the red oak, the one with the
swing tied to it. Hard to even begin.

They slept late, and when they woke up, the day was innocent
– chilly suddenly, and less complicated. The humidity was gone
and the pumpkins on the hill were about two tones brighter than
the day before. Caroline's mother had made grape juice from the
fat, sweet muscadines and Misty said, "that looks like blood," but
it didn't at all – it was splashy and dark pink, maybe a dream
where blood turns out to be harmless.

They decided to go spy on RaeAnn, who had to work at the
produce stand, now that she was a Sluder. In order to make
something happen, they had to get closer to her than what they
could see from their lookout. If they found her alone in just the
right way, they could warn her what to expect. She might be
so grateful she would help them: a piece of Lance's shirt was
the most they needed, to make the doll. Only a little square of
flannel.

Caroline took a dollar of her own allowance money, a
crumpled bill from her old music box, the one with the little
ballerina on top who still pirouetted drunkenly when you raised
the lid. Outside again, the girls cut around the dying garden.
Wild milkweed loomed over the guardrail that separated the
land from the country highway.

The sky had been cleaned by a blue eraser. Lance wasn't
flying the Ultralight, so they could hear what sounded like a

single bug, down from the whole chorus – just one cricket frantic at some hidden microphone in the ditch.

There she was. RaeAnn was there – they saw her behind the Sluder Family Produce stand with its hand-lettered sign and its jars of canned tomatoes and relish and five kinds of jam, the ears of the last corn and the last redskin potatoes and the very, very last beefsteak tomatoes all stacked up.

RaeAnn looked small and vulnerable, exactly as they had gone to find her. They saw she was wearing a long-sleeved sweatshirt. Hiding bruises? Lance was so big – he was certainly bigger than Caroline's father. Misty had said he was probably bigger than her father, too, although her father, who was divorced from her mother, was very tall and also quite tough. But Lance was tough, too. And RaeAnn's whole charm was in those tiny wrists she had, and a neck as frail as a dandelion stem anyone could kick in half.

"Hey, girls," she said. "Big excitement here this morning. A weasel after the chickens. You just missed it."

The girls said "ohhh" together. Caroline gave RaeAnn the dollar, smoothed straight, pointed to a pile of ears, and watched her carelessly weigh up the corn. Was the weasel RaeAnn's fault?

"Did it bite anybody?" asked Misty.

Caroline removed her thumb cuticle from her teeth. "Why was it out during the day?"

"That's a good question, hon," said RaeAnn. *We're neighbors,* thought Caroline. *Of course she would like me more.*

RaeAnn wasn't scared – she was, Caroline realized, the princess of weasels. Anyone would want to marry her. "Maybe rabid. Lance got it with a shovel, didn't even take time to shoot it."

Caroline made a blind move. As hard as she could in her flip-flop, she stepped on Misty's sneaker: a filthy Ked. Her movement was hidden from RaeAnn by the thick safety of the produce stand.

She stayed on her friend's foot, grinding it slowly into the ground. Her bony hip found Misty's real one. She felt the voodoo doll, undressed and inadequate, trapped in the hem of Misty's terry-cloth shorts.

"Was it really rabies, or just distemper?" Misty asked. Again a thief: she had learned the distinction from Caroline. Both diseases made the animal lurch and foam. But humans couldn't catch distemper.

"God knows," said RaeAnn. Her hair was permed and very long, heavier than her head. Caroline wondered who was taking care of RaeAnn's horse, abandoned now with no girl there to love him into existence.

"We wanted to know," Misty started. Caroline gouged her cuticles and looked at the ground. The heat of the summer came back; it had traveled to her face.

Misty stopped. Then she started again: "So, we wanted to ask you something?" Caroline heard, almost for the first time, how out of place Misty was with her meddling. Grinding her gears. There might be no way, ever, to sew up the distance between city and country.

"Is everything okay with you? Are you all right?" Misty looked at the ground after she said it. *Your shame does you credit; I find it an improvement*, Caroline thought in her British accent. She took the paper bag of corn from RaeAnn and hid her own face behind it.

When they dared to look up again, RaeAnn was raising a single eyebrow. So she was talented, too. "You girls better run along," she said. "I'm pretty busy here."

"She didn't want to talk about it," Misty said.

"He used a shovel," said Caroline. "That is pure brutality." They went into their overlook and sat down on their crates in the seedy grass. The walnuts were green and dropping – an odor like fake lime. The spell book was still there, rotten with dew, and they muttered a few incantations together, the easiest bits they could find.

Then they climbed as far as they could in the tree without getting dizzy. They chucked the voodoo doll, just as it was, nude and powerless, over the property line into the Sluder fields.

Of course it was Leif who ended up with it, who even began carrying it around like a little pet. A voodoo doll with no magic was even less than a regular doll. They found it on him soon enough.

It was Misty's last two days to be in the country before school began. Both their schools would start again next week, and Misty didn't seem concerned about this but Caroline, up in her room, lying on her bed under the low eaves, fumbled sixth grade around like a cat's-eye marble.

She wondered who might be sitting beside her this year, pictured how amazed her teacher would be when she found out Caroline had forced her way through *Wuthering Heights* in June and July – all that absurd, violent bluster during her freest months. She had kept the confounding characters straight, all those names exactly the same, and could express herself in the manner of any old foreign book, if called upon to do so.

She picked up items in her pile of school supplies and smoothed them with an inrush of sweetness – a five-subject notebook with a hard blue cover, a pink vinyl pencil case with a pleasing chemical smell. She didn't run, right away, when she heard the metallic, old-fashioned doorbell clutter the peace of her parents' house.

Was this her only friend, after all? The noise kept on and she huffed wearily, stomping down the big staircase with no one in hearing distance to tell her not to do it. The wooden banister was so old it was starting to shake a little. Caroline trailed the smudge of dust all the way down and put her finger into her mouth.

She didn't let Misty in. Instead, she joined her on the front porch, where they both sat on the steps, scratching their knees and watching trucks fan hugely by on the narrow two-lane highway.

Most of the trucks hauled long, steel livestock trailers behind them. They could just see the wet noses of cattle, pressed hopeless as stars against the air slits. They were on their way to the slaughterhouse.

"What do you want to do today?" asked Misty. "Why didn't you come down right away?"

Caroline opened her mouth to answer but swallowed an explosion instead, a hell boom they thought at first was thunder – out of another perfect sky. Their gasps came in late, but that was just shock. Otherwise silence. Even the birds shut up. Then they saw a gurgle of smoke above the treeline, turning black. Somewhere, far out of sight, RaeAnn began to scream.

It was possible that Lance wouldn't die – that he would live but was just paralyzed. Or it was possible he wasn't paralyzed at all but only had two broken legs, one shattered and the other fractured, and would be up and around again by Christmas.

Labor Day weekend had changed for everyone, that was certain. Caroline's father drove his big Buick over to the Sluder farm, stayed a while to visit, and brought back news. The Ultralight was ruined – it didn't have enough weight to it to survive a crash.

The Sluders were bound to comfort the broken man, so Caroline and Misty were given a job, watching Leif while the rest of the family stayed at the hospital, waiting for updates. They warmed to his care. Caroline poured Leif a glass of grape juice and cut the corners off a peanut-butter-and-jelly sandwich for him, serving him there in her own kitchen. Misty was even better: she played with him for hours.

Misty and Leif were building a house out of a deck of old cards, the one with bald eagles printed on the backs, left over from the Bicentennial. Misty got up, her ponytail at rest, and tiptoed over to close the tall windows – as though they belonged to her – so the light September wind wouldn't blow the cards over. Everything was changed.

Leif was so good at it; he was really so much better at it than they were that they had to admit it, and leave him alone to finish. He was deadly meticulous. By the time his sister-in-law came to pick him back up, it was getting close to supper time, and Leif had constructed his card house without a flaw.

It was higher than his own body. It was still standing – he was standing inside of it.

"That's the best card house in the world," said Caroline. She whispered so the house wouldn't blow over. "You could be in the Guinness Book."

"Do you do this all the time when you're at home?" Misty asked. Her bold prettiness made Leif shy. Or it didn't. He said nothing.

The explosion – exhilarating – and suddenly this little alien to care for – it was oddly festive. And then RaeAnn came into it all, extra as a holiday. Another stranger in the house. Caroline's mother led her to them, murmuring this and that about her injured husband. She told RaeAnn that Leif was holding up very well.

"He hasn't gotten upset or been any kind of trouble," said Caroline's mother. "Just playing quietly with the girls. He's really a darling boy."

RaeAnn had been crying, though. Her eyelashes dripped in Caroline's living room – a room heavy with vine-pattern drapes, dominated by the dark grand piano.

"I see he's got that disgusting thing again," said RaeAnn, pointing to the soggy, disfigured stump of clay. Caroline and Misty had encouraged Leif to set the voodoo doll on top of the piano, leaning against the metronome, where they could adore it together.

"You little freak," said RaeAnn. "Always embarrassing us." Leif didn't look up; he was still setting up cards with his precise burrowing gestures.

"Lance used that plane to get away," RaeAnn said. Her voice struck around the room – their best room, full of antiques. Caroline was frozen, trying to catch her friend's eye. But more than Misty's attention, she wanted her mother, who was still in the shadows, making little moans of protest.

RaeAnn moved swiftly, whacked the card house with the side of her dainty hand. It just didn't take much to bring it down. "Lance is critically injured, Leif," she said. "Look at me for once, dummy. He has a body cast on." She spit out the last sentence – grapes hitting the metal colander. The little boy stood, the cards fluttering down around him.

"Will he walk again?" This came from Misty. She was as harmless now as the fields after they stripped them of pumpkins. Soft and done for. Caroline blushed – but who was it for? *I was once frightened of you*, Caroline mouthed in her accent.

"Lance used that plane to get away," RaeAnn said again.

"Let's all keep our heads," said Caroline's mother, as her daughter tiptoed over to get the lonely doll. The least Caroline could do – she could hide it from RaeAnn – get it away from those killing eyes. She would keep it a while, then get it back to Leif. Right now, someone needed protection, no time to ask why.

Nicki the Namer

Mrs. Ballantine had almost finalized her choices for the coming twins, but as her hired baby namer, it behooved me to keep her feeling unsure until the very end. She was a lady of privilege, Mrs. Ballantine: a petite worrier with a platinum ponytail, yoga tank cinched up like an old corset to reveal her harrowing, unlikely belly. Me, I had my good collection of broomstick skirts and peasant blouses, and no one touched my own hair but me. Usually I did it in Dutch braids, tightly twisted whips falling down to my waist.

Mrs. Ballantine and I were both forty-seven years old. She had a house cleaner she called a good friend; one day soon she would have a nanny. I painted scenery and sewed costumes for the community theatre in between my paying gigs, and my apartment was one of eight in an old firetrap of a Victorian house: little more than a sleeping porch and a kitchenette.

But we fell in step. Mrs. Ballantine was a person who prostrated herself at the altar of expertise, and there I was, knowing exactly how many queens named Catherine had sat on the thrones of Europe since 1401.

Mr. Ballantine didn't get why this was delightful, so mostly we avoided him during the naming discussions. He used my own first name too often, too earnestly, like this whole operation was unfolding peer to peer. But his wife was in thrall to my courtly formality. She was nervous by nature, and being called "Mrs." settled something inside her. Toward the end of our time together, before her girls were born, she and I met for coffee once a week to refine our list. I would order a caramel Frappuccino with whipped cream and Mrs. Ballantine would get an herbal tea, always clucking with disappointment over the limited menu, and on every visit, we gave the barista two new baby names.

Easing off to the waiting queue, we would look drolly at one another. I'd put a finger up to my lips, dramatically, and Mrs. Ballantine would make a zipping motion across hers. We had to be quiet until they called out our orders, so we could feel the names resonate in real time.

At first, Mrs. Ballantine favored pairs of popular names like Stella and Ava, Sophie and Lucy. For one alarming week she stalled out on Emma and Olivia. *They have that old-fashioned ring that really appeals to me,* she said, and I had to close my eyes a beat. She couldn't come up with any middle names beyond Rose and Grace. But since she was paying me $75 an hour, I had to be patient with her ignorance. I printed off a list from the Social Security Administration website and marked it up with red pen on the live-edge writing desk in her home office, where she had set me an ergonomic chair. The previous year, Emma had been the number one girls' name in America. Olivia was number three. *That's a whole lot of Emmas,* I told her, *and a whole lot of Olivias. Picture what kindergarten might be like for them.*

Once an old-fashioned name became hot again, it lost all traces of its original context, I explained to Mrs. Ballantine. She needed to dig deeper if she wanted to go the vintage route. The Ballantines had TVs like movie screens mounted in five rooms of their mountaintop home, so when I produced my most recent list of baby girls' names, I included some that had been popping up among celebrity parents, and as style names for small-batch designer sundresses. I asked her to consider Hattie and Celia, or Flora and Lottie, or Evelyn and Lucretia. *These names would have been unthinkable five or ten years ago,* I said. *But today they sound fresh as daisies.*

She should have already known. After all, the Ballantines had moved here from California. They'd come back to be closer to east coast relatives but still have views to post: instead of fog and bay, it was black bears in the garbage cans and blue hills furrowing back to divinity. Neither one of them had to be anywhere in particular, even for work, and their money was so new it was practically raw.

When Mr. Ballantine texted me, he always wrote "it is." *How are you? It is a lovely day.* And I would text back: *Why, yes, it is. It is indeed a lovely day.* He wasn't a foreigner or a gentleman; he just didn't know whether to use "its" or "it's." The only books I ever saw on Mrs. Ballantine's custom built-in bookshelves had simpleminded titles that nevertheless needed long, fussy subtitles to explain the first ones. *French Country Fresh: Exciting New Ways to Get the Classic French Country Look in Your Home and Garden.*

So I hoped she was too sophisticated to consider rhyming names, or, just as unseemly, names starting with the same letter.

I'm sure you know that's a dated practice, I said. *Dated in a bad way, I mean.* And she said: *Oh, of course. Of course, of course.*

I held her in place with my raised eyebrow.

Well, anyway, she said, *they're fraternal.*

Really, we lived in a great big country, and naming choices had multiplied so much in the past twenty years there wasn't much chance of her girls running into someone with the same first name, never mind all those Emmas and Olivias. This I kept to myself. But if I had decided to tell her, I would have said: *It wasn't like in our day, with Jennifers lurking around every corner. I remember we had so many Jens in my middle school they had to form their own club.*

My own first name hit number ten the year I was born, and my caregivers shortened it to its least effectual form before I even had a say in the matter. It was flaky and common, and I had often thought of changing it to something that felt more like me – Magdalene, Desdemona. But now, at least, it had the same first letter as "Namer." The alliteration would serve me well in my branding efforts.

My dream gig began with a glorious prize. A couple summers back, I'd gone to a local lavender festival on Hominy Mountain with my two friends from the theatre, Kirk and Mitchell. None of us were particularly outdoorsy – not like Mrs. Ballantine, who did yoga outside if it was above forty degrees, and certainly not like Mr. Ballantine, who spent his weekends grinding against age and gravity on a Yeti mountain bike.

But Hominy Mountain could lure anyone. It was a sunny bald that swelled like a parachute between the more distant hills. Because it was one of the mile-high mountains, it had a *Sound of Music* look – more meadowy than the lower peaks, which were throttled with haze and foliage – and sort of a rarefied silence. You couldn't get that feeling below five thousand feet.

Also, with all the lavender, we could pretend we were in Provence.

It was the third week of June, but the wind still had a chill. *I need y'all to guess how much a Yeti mountain bike costs*, I said to Kirk and Mitchell, tightening my fringed paisley shawl around my shoulders.

Kirk said something snarky about Bigfoot finally getting his training wheels, but I was out of breath from climbing the last quarter mile, steep and full of roots, where the car wouldn't go, which meant I was also out of patience with his wit. So I said, *They're eleven-thousand dollars. Without extras.*

Why'd you tell us to guess then? said Kirk.

That's more than my car, said Mitchell, drooping.

We all had our plans. I wanted to buy stalks of lavender so I could dry out the buds and sew them up inside something, maybe a sweet sachet to keep in my camisole drawer. I wanted some of the farm's homemade lavender soaps to put in the iron soap dish in my clawfoot tub. Mitchell had a digital camera around his neck; he was trying to break into landscape photography as a side hustle. Kirk was just bored, as usual, and hungover.

We came into a clearing, encountering a tanned older hippie with the silver version of my braids who was sitting at a card table with pamphlets and a big glass jug. She told us all the donations collected benefitted the farm, which was, of course, a nonprofit. She said *not-for-profit.*

The thin sun struck her in the face, and I couldn't see her eyes behind her glasses. Kirk, who was artistic director at the theatre, started in about the various headaches of nonprofit life. Five minutes in and he was already wheeling his arms around like a big-time agitator. Mitchell was looking anxiously at a carpet of purple, swaying clumps off to our right – it was the lavender field, crawling dimly with bees. He cursed himself for something.

I clutched his arm. *You remembered your Epi Pen, yes?*

Yes, he said. *I just didn't realize the extent of the orgy.*

But then, wandering around, I saw bigger animals on display and forgot about Kirk and Mitchell. It appeared they were donkeys: six of them were stubby, either young animals or miniature ones – or maybe donkeys were just apt to be short. But the seventh one was white and startlingly large, like a unicorn. They were crowded in a temporary-looking pen at the side of an old barn. Someone had written a sign by hand.

Help Us Name our Rescue Donkeys!
Hominy Mountain Lavender Farm is now expanding our
outreach to care for what we feel is the most misunderstood

of all four-legged farm animals, the humble and hardworking Donkey. These neglected beauties came to us named after the Seven Dwarfs, and we think our visitors can do better. Write your choice of seven new names on one of the slips below and put it in the cardboard box. Don't forget to include your own name and phone number! The white one and the one with the injured ear are male and the rest are female. The lucky winner will get a gift basket of lovingly crafted lavender goodies.

I spread my shawl out on the grass and sank to the ground, settling myself cross-legged. *I believe you mean Dwarves,* I muttered to the fragrant air. Then I went into a kind of trance, gazing into the donkeys' sneering devout faces. I knew the prize was mine to win; I felt the mission had been delivered to me personally. Humming "The Schuyler Sisters" from *Hamilton,* I got my pencil and paper from an old soup can they had wired to the pen. I breathed deep from my diaphragm and let the donkeys' individual characters flow into me.

I wrote the names in a column. A scroll.

Dulcie.
Prudence.
Shasta.
Rizzio.
Clementine.

Those were the girls. The saddest one, the one with the bad ear, was, naturally, Vincent. The unicorn donkey was Edelweiss.

Apparently the contest had been going on the whole weekend, and I made my friends wait there with me all afternoon until the winner was announced. We had taken my car, so I had them trapped. Kirk got sunburned and stopped speaking to me, and even Mitchell began to lose his cool a little, forgetting every ten minutes there wasn't a signal up this high and stabbing at his phone to try to reach civilization.

It was muggy, that night, back in the valley. No matter, though: I was the victor. I propped up my thick, dangerous, antique window with a paint stirrer and lay back on my white iron bed, against my float of tapestry pillows, and opened my laptop. Discreetly, I smoked a Dunhill, blowing the smoke out the window. I drank a chalice of red wine and ate the cupcakes with medicinal-tasting lavender icing that had come in my prize basket.

My own rescues, my three cats, lay at my head and feet. Hush was deaf, Lucifer had had the black fur on his face burned off by firecrackers, and Indira, formerly known as Shadow, had come to me morbidly shy. But now she stretched in my direction, twisting her small head into the glow shed by Facebook, and I paused to massage her upturned chin with my knuckle. Having announced my win, I set about creating a page for my newest enterprise: professional baby-naming services.

Dwight wasn't allowed to speak without permission, and if he dared to address me, he had to use the proper appellation: Lady Portia. He most certainly wasn't allowed to touch me, nor himself, during our sessions together, and my payment was secured beforehand, tucked in an envelope and sitting on a side table inside the front door of his mobile home. I counted the money slowly, fanning it out. Stalling was important, for dramatic suspense – but sometimes I just hadn't had time to prepare a script for the hour.

It took some effort to stay in character with Dwight. I was resourceful, I had always been so; I was hard as a knitting needle inside and proud to have gotten that way – but I wasn't a monster.

He was the same age as me, or thereabouts, but already he had an oxygen tube living in his nose. He had grown too wide and too weak to mind his hygiene, and to hide my disgust at his oily ponytail and his stained sweatpants, his buzzing about in that motorized chair like it meant any kind of momentum, my eyes would shift to the oval-framed photos lined up just so on his paneled wall, this proof of hope and verve stuffed far out of the sun.

There was a little Dwight, appearing punchy and sweet in a grade-school photo, his buffalo-plaid shirt clean and pressed. There he was with his parents and an older sister at Disney World, all four of them wearing the same mouse ears. There was a wedding photo taken so long ago the bride wore a rhinestone banana clip. The most recent portrait showed Dwight cuddling a curly white puppy; that dog was now sour-tempered, yellow, and kept in a crate during my visits.

My one concession to the style of a classic dominatrix was a pair of high black boots: wide-calved and made of vegan leather. But I never exposed my breasts, which were monumental, goddess-given – in fact, my pinstriped shirt numbered seventy-five buttons up to a ruffled chin and might have been worn by a Victorian schoolmistress. I had sewn my own black velvet mini skirt and matching cape; I was unrecognizable in my harlequin half mask, and I trusted that no one but me carried a hand-braided willow switch rather than some bullwhip or riding crop bought cheaply online.

Today I painted Dwight's foul animal toenails a candy pink, knowing he wouldn't be able to reach down to remove the polish. I embellished gravely on all of his failures to please, his evidence of absolute worthlessness. I kept my voice level and resigned as a judge, then raised it throatily, threatening perilous beatings if he failed to agree with me after every fresh insult.

Yes, Lady Portia, he said. *You know best, Lady Portia. Just as you say, Lady Portia. Oh, thank you, Lady Portia.*

Dwight kept his eyes closed, and his breathing changed, growing not faster but instead slowing down – laden with a kind of peace. I was always bemused to observe his long feminine lashes, the improbable bloom in his cheeks.

But I struck his hands hard enough to leave red marks. He was to keep them in my sight at all times, turned palm up in the agreed-upon submissive gesture.

Every moment, until the hour was up, I worried he would die in my keep. I took to turning my car around in his driveway, pointing at the road for a smoother getaway. During our early back-and-forth, our initial conversations through the fetish website, he wrote in a shy, almost self-congratulatory way about his failing health, the torment of his secret yearnings, and in passing he mentioned that his sister checked in on him once a week, always the same day at the same time, he assured me. No chance of a run-in.

But I couldn't risk getting trapped, and especially by someone of her presumed ignorance. I didn't have time to explain myself to a court of any kind, to all those who would say I was exploiting Dwight's condition, perhaps endangering his life.

I came cheaper than a nurse, is what I figured. I came cheaper than a therapist, too, and from what I saw, from what Dwight conveyed to me himself, over and over, I was second only to that stinking, beloved dog in alleviating his misery.

The wealthy men, being all the same, never stayed long on my mind once the business was over. They wriggled in endless liberty inside those caverns of theirs – featureless quasi-mansions furnished in shades of bone, impressive only for their lack of echo. With these men, the transactions lost more of their gray areas. If the houses seemed interchangeable, so did the clients and their situations. The wives were always reported to be out shopping or at a weekly luncheon with friends, or else busy-busy, doing good at their volunteer positions, light years away from suspecting a thing, and maybe that far from caring, too.

I tried to keep feeling superior about all the bland neutral furniture in these houses, the walls made of windows that sucked in a gluttonous portion of natural light. In every kitchen was a prep island as big as a pleasure boat, but no evidence of meals recently enjoyed.

The master bedroom was usually situated on the main level, in the mountain-modern style, but so far away from the common living area there was time enough to ponder the history of class warfare on the journey there. Once I had them where I wanted them, the wealthy husbands emerged in their most authentic light: still arrogant, but suddenly fragile. They were usually over sixty but occasionally as old as eighty, and it was frankly crushing, how glad they always were to see me.

One of them had a bed frame carved to look like marble; the obscene beveled posts reached almost to the ceiling. *A feat of form and function*, this client couldn't resist whispering, a braggart even with his concave chest and his sagging silk boxers, holding his wrists against a column to be tied.

When I recounted some of these sessions to my two friends, Kirk would go rapt. Naturally I never named names, just paused for effect when I wanted to shock, maybe steepled my fingers and slow-blinked. That's all I had to do to convulse him in laughter – he was everyone's dream listener. He scrubbed away tears with the heel of his hand; he told me I would be wise to buy a handgun and learn how to use it.

Mitchell was different. He only shook his head, smiled sadly, or sometimes allowed himself a paternal *tsk*. He said he hoped I remembered to write down all these lurid details for my future memoirs. Mitchell was one of about three people alive from whom I would accept a hug.

Maybe I was just an old-fashioned prude, maybe that was my issue, though I had had lovers enough, over the years, beginning in high school – and me a tall, heavy Goth girl who might have been an outcast, at least by the standards of my day. But a large body draped in black clothing didn't seem to matter in my case, because even at sixteen, I knew only confidence mattered. I kept my head up, I kept a cape on from the beginning, and I led my own world, portioning out my attention exactly so: like a world leader.

But being also a mountain-born girl, I was practical. I knew where my preening ran into its own limit. Gradually, in hard-won bits, I got through college, then went even further with it and obtained my Master's degree in English Literature. I was burdened with a student loan to pay off, but even so, I never entered the world of academia, where I probably belonged.

I never became a teacher – it was because I didn't want to be caught at the front of a classroom, pinned to death by sixty eyes. I wanted to do the looking myself, not be the thing considered.

I could sew, I could paint, I read as consumingly as some batty prisoner, and I wrote a salty music-review column in my city's alternative newsweekly, under the name Zara X. Lemmon. My readers waited for Zara's opinion; no other freelancer on the paper's payroll could accumulate so many comments.

I always knew what I did not want: any overbearing man or unpredictable children to rip open the stitched-together scraps of my tranquility. So freed, I defaulted on my single duty, the loan, and gathered up enough side money, this one year, for a plane ticket to England. I divined that it was just as doable as that. For a week I walked, and rode buses and trains, visiting the Tower of London and the Globe Theatre and Jane Austen's house in Chawton.

I learned that the brand-new Jane had been sent away from home as an infant, reared by a wet nurse for a year and a half before being returned to her rightful family, and still she grew up to the business of genius like none of it mattered at all. I learned this fact – it was mild fare, well documented – and I could not forget it.

I met nine-month-old Jacoby Tristan when I was shopping for a vial of myrrh in the body-care department of our city's natural-foods market. Right there, stuffed thoughtfully inside an organic cotton baby sling, he looked straight into my eyes and flashed me a wizard's smile. His mother chattered on about all the unique ways Jacoby had been entertaining his family since I'd named him *in utero* – for example, spitting out his pacifier while one or the other of his parents were driving and couldn't pause to retrieve it. He spit it out so hard it would hit the inside of the Land Rover's back windshield.

I couldn't coo in the manner of accomplished sentimental people, but I winked at him, marveling at this violently beautiful thing I had created.

Dashiell Matthias' mother thought to text me a photo of him at three weeks, wide awake and frowning, brooding about the world – a deep thinker, just as I knew he would be when I named him. And it was easy to keep tabs on D'arcy Sigrún, a dainty baby born to a public life: her parents had a profitable business turning well-to-do breast-cancer survivors into adventuresses. They sold these women trips to Iceland, where they mounted them on shaggy Icelandic horses and trotted them up and down black-sand beaches for a spell of two weeks. The riders were encouraged to post daily updates about their gratitude.

D'arcy Sigrún's parents were too dedicated to let a baby interfere with this brilliant life, so they merely brought her along with them as though nothing out of the way had occurred by her being born. In the ersatz pulse of an Instagram photo, festively arrayed in a Fair Isle sweater and matching beanie, my girl pursed her mouth around a spoonful of Icelandic *skyr* and appeared to be safe in her element.

It was futile to hope. By now I knew better. But didn't great skill secure its own dividends? When all of these babies – these expressive wee animals who owed me the first spell of their lives, their own fledgling selfhoods – began showing up in real time, snug inside themselves and growing, thriving, I started daydreaming that the naming gig alone might support me, and I could give up the other thing.

I would no longer have to picture needy, beatific Dwight slipping out of life in his motorized chair. Nor would I need to puzzle out the quickest exit route from some CEO's museum-sized vacation house, lived in half the year.

In one fantasy, I found a bit of land to rent – anything with a shack on it would do – and coaxed Edelweiss away from the people at the lavender farm. I would bring him home to the place he truly belonged: safe with me.

I wasn't really any better than the parents of D'arcy Sigrún: I imagined blogging about about my life with Edelweiss, post upon post, me the acclaimed professional namer, the ultimate haughty cat lady, the intimidating, eloquent mother of a magical unicorn donkey, all of us living cranky and wild, famous but free.

But first I had to stop Mr. Ballantine. His texts were growing more and more pointed in the weeks leading up to his twin daughters' due date. The tone was sometimes managerial, efficient with hollow praise – the way he might speak to an employee of his mysterious IT company.

You have been an important part of our journey. We truly appreciate your services.

More often, his messages were simply creepy and jovial. At all times, they were unnecessary, since he really didn't seem to care much what his children would be called, nor how much money it was costing to name them, as long as Mrs. Ballantine had me to help absorb some of her nervous affliction. At bottom, it was a loopy species of loneliness no one wanted to catch.

I never asked what role fertility treatments had played in the creation of this family. All Mrs. Ballantine ever offered was the tale of her wedding, seven years before: she and Mr. Ballantine hadn't found one another until she was forty years old and he was fifty, she explained one day at the coffee shop. Because of their ages, she said, naturally they were compelled to make a big splash. They picked Memorial Day weekend and flew to Saint-Tropez. It was a true elopement, according to Mrs. Ballantine. They told no one beforehand. That situation was made all the sweeter when they posted the sun-drenched evidence to their world of followers.

How fabulous, I said. *I'm picturing a vintage Vanity Fair spread.*

She squeezed my arm, then put her hand back on her greatly distended belly. With her other hand, she picked up one of my own hands and placed it on the other side of the belly. Small as she was everywhere else, it appeared by now she had swallowed a bewitched melon. The Great Pumpkin. An out-of-control tumor begun in a test tube, a teacup.

An old Irish saying popped into my head: *Marry in May, rue the day.* Of course, I didn't say it out loud.

I was the mistress of minding my own business, perhaps even the Doyenne of Disguise – and so far, it had not made me rich. But it did make people depend on me, somehow, even hang on my word. At his insistence, I finally agreed to meet Mr. Ballantine alone, without Mrs. Ballantine in the house. He said he needed to tie up a few key points with me before his world changed forever.

It is going to be a sea change, he texted. *Fatherhood at fifty-seven was never something I imagined for my self.*

Indeed, I wrote back. *But let's meet at Starbucks, shall we? The big one on your side of town. That's where Mrs. B. likes to go to test out baby names with me. I'm sure she must have mentioned it.*

But he said he was most comfortable in his own home, since he had something important to discuss with me. A bit of a secret.

So I got in my little car. I drove through town and past town and eventually parted the gates of their community – naturally Mrs. Ballantine had given me the code months ago.

I curved around immaculately paved roads that some sharp developer had named after the native flora of Southern Appalachia: *Ladyslipper Lane, Flame Azalea Road, Woodsorrel Way, Trillium Trail.* On and on, then up and up to their house, which was always a shock when it came into view. It was three storeys high, built of stacked fieldstone, no lawn, anchored off a ridge with steel beams. It looked like a castle that had jumped its own moat.

I met him in the part of their house they called the Outdoor Room, a covered deck that contained more square footage than my apartment. The space was flush with amenities, all of them scaled for a duchy: rustic ceiling beams reclaimed from various demolished antique churches, a gas grill bigger than a bear and surrounded by another spread of river rock, retractable floor-to-ceiling window screens that worked by remote control, and a rapacious one-hundred-and-eighty degree view of what were supposed to be our mountains. The mountains belonging to all of the people.

Mr. Ballantine poured me a Moscow Mule in a hammered copper cup and brandished it at me dramatically; he could name the local artisan who had made it. I said, *Now, this truly IS a chalice*, and I was only murmuring, but he asked me to repeat myself, and he laughed and even blushed against his wavy, salt-and-pepper hair, and once again, as I had for months now, I tried to divine what this couple had been doing their entire lives to have remained so innocent, so easily pleased – so quickly seduced by an uncommon word.

I pretended I was there to talk names, as though he were finally coming around to the proper interest, now that he almost a father. I revealed to him what Mrs. Ballantine and I were calling our Final Four: *Cora Bronwen, Frankie Matilda, Delaney Niamh*, and *Aisling Ruth*.

Delaney What? he said. I told him that Mrs. Ballantine had developed a sudden fondness, in this last stretch, for what she considered to be Celtic names. I'd had to introduce some truly traditional options and steer her away from her first round of ideas.

Erin is too American, I explained to him now, as I had to her. It had become a recitation. *Maggie is only colloquially Irish, though it does have a history in our local ballad culture. Bridget hasn't come back into vogue, but it might have possibilities in a few years. And Caitlin is close to the actual word for "girl" in Irish, but it's been way watered down.* Feeling inspired, I added: *It was the most common cheerleader's name in 2005.*

His blue eyes shifted around. He nodded off beat, drumming his manicured nails on his matching copper chalice. Mrs. Ballantine was attending a Prenatal Yoga session with a new acquaintance, he repeated.

There he was, finally emerging, finished with the tedium of identity. I was obliged to nudge my drink away.

Following a spell of nothing, I said, *I'm glad to hear she's found a friend to share her experience more authentically.* Mr. Ballantine reminded me that Mrs. Ballantine's C-section was scheduled in seven days.

Staying smooth, I handed Mr. Ballantine the receiving blankets I had sewn for the baby girls, wrapped individually in tissue paper inside a recycled grocery bag. One was cornflower blue with mustard-colored wildflowers, and the other was mint green with champagne-colored *fleur-de-lis*. Not a hint of pink in sight.

Ours was a small city – to people like them, it was only a town – but we all lived such remote lives, every human a separate star, that I never knew how Mr. Ballantine found out about me. What he wanted me to do wasn't even in my official repertoire, but he flattered me, and he named an outrageous number, and I sat there in someone else's rich, thick breeze and made a grown-up choice.

About a month later, I came back to the house at Mrs. Ballantine's invitation to view the newborns. She inhabited the Outdoor Room in her bespoke Scandinavian nursing rocker, dressed in a long white gown like a real Victorian and looking not new and transformed in her longed-for role but stunned, ossified, a swaddled bundle settled on each of her toned arms, which were gamely bearing the burden. I detected a faint trembling, but I couldn't tell whether it came from her body or theirs. Maybe the babies were set to go off like old-fashioned alarm clocks.

I learned that Cora Bronwen was the bigger twin by an entire pound. It was comforting to look at her stout, moony face. Frankie Matilda was narrower, faintly jaundiced. As I gazed down at her, she jerked inside some minute infant dream. She would require the most strength in that family. Or she would lead it.

I whispered in Mrs. Ballantine's ear, deadly quiet so as not to wake the babies. *Don't be afraid to call them by their full names. This is the South, after all, and you're a real Southerner now,* I lied gently. *Double names are bound to come back in style.*

She smiled up at me. *I can't see any reason why they shouldn't,* I added. She rocked and rocked and seemed to hold the babies closer. I patted her slim shoulder and told her how very well she had done.

Killing Frost

January dropped. A bitter, smudgy snow locked the town down for a week. Only the ones with serious four-wheel-drive vehicles and a lot more ambition than we had could get out.

Me and Colby, we needed to get over some hump we couldn't even see. I was still living in the band house because I had a room in a turret and because the landlord, an eloquent creep named Boozer, liked me – I was the only girl, so he gave me a secret cut on the rent.

Boozer lived a long, twisting drive away in the next county. The rumor was, he had a grow operation in a one-time tobacco barn, sheltered down in some holler. That's where he'd gotten the cash to buy this place in town, a Queen Anne Victorian right there on Main Street. It was at least a hundred years old, all dormers and dingy frills. Boozer had a scent: green gone to hell.

He'd once had a wife, but it was more natural for him to have nobody.

Poor Colby, though. My little friend! He'd become so dispensable. Messing with his sequencer for hours, trying to record other people's music but not at all musical himself. He'd worked his way up to being the front-end manager at the New Age Market down on Second Avenue and Cox, a place run by a prudish family of hippies.

Colby was always testing out his personality, and that job promotion, it made him officious. He became more clean-cut. I watched him shave off the last of his gingery beard in one of the Queen Anne's three bathrooms, the oldest one original to the house.

The bathroom had a clawfoot tub. Underneath it, the olive linoleum sagged. It was like the tub intended not only to crash into the floor below it, but into a better century. The mountain light, kingly in winter, pushed through the transom window.

I was sitting on the toilet, a mug of black coffee wrapped in both of my hands – a bunch of sugar, no milk – watching Colby have his moment with that razor. *Scrape. Scrape.* I winced when he bumped it over his Adam's apple.

I would pee in front of any of the guys, we were that comfortable – but I was waiting to be alone to let out anything more; I had been working on my boundaries now for a couple of years.

The house needed so much fixing. By fall, the gutters were filling up. By winter they were suffocated. No one had touched the yard all season and it was all too late – the poison oak and kudzu had choked out the flowers and strangled the weeping cherry tree. Only a spooky old locust leaning into my turret window seemed to thrive. Bare-branched, now, in winter. But alive.

Boozer begged. He claimed he would take any yardwork or home improvements we did off the rent. Really, the place was as disgusting as it was magnificent.

The other guys loved Colby like a mascot but hated him, too, called him a little bitch. A little prick. Always little: he was about as tall as me. I didn't hate him. I was exempt from theatrics.

I had never tried to be in the band. It was never appealing to me, the notion of so much compromise. Every night a late night. I was a decently read college graduate with a useless degree, and I crafted together dangly earrings out of silver wire and sold them at craft markets April through December. Also, I babysat houses. They were the vacation homes of the middle-aged Yuppies, empty most of the year, cheap A-frames clinging to slopes on the ridge.

Architecture wasn't a thing yet. I got by.

"Let's go see that new shop before your shift," I said, bending my head down. I used the point of my tongue to stir my coffee in a counter-clockwise fashion. "We need to check this place out."

"Ooh! It's a plan," he said. The shop was called *Ooh! La La Boutique: Fine Consignments.* The sign was hand painted, and the punctuation troubling. "Ooh" was right, but that exclamation mark – the passion was all off-center.

It was the best part of our week. We said "Ooh!" a couple times every hour.

We were stranded. Colby's Moped needed a part, and my asthmatic Ford Escort was drifted over and no good in the snow, anyway. We walked, or we concocted sled rides down the steepest of the streets, using flattened cardboard, mostly beer cases. We scraped up handfuls of change from under the house's couches and chairs to buy a couple dark pints at the bar, or a sandwich to split at the coffee house, or a double cappuccino to pass between us.

Today would be better. I had cash from the Christmas craft shows and Colby had just been put on some kind of salary.

For weeks, the owner of Ooh! La La had made trips up and down Main, driving carefree even when the roads turned slippery. Her new Subaru had boxes inside it and strapped on top of it, the way a local might haul a dinged-up kayak or camping gear.

I kept wearing the olive cardigan and white T-shirt and corduroy pants I had been loitering in forever, and my favorite slouchy beanie and llama-print red-and-white mittens and the Navy-issue pea coat with three missing buttons, and a pair of combat boots I couldn't give up even though they were too small and made my pinkie toes go dead. Colby had L.L.Bean boots that his mother had probably mailed him. He looked like an asshole in a wool beret, especially paired with a ski vest, but I gripped his arm to steady him as we skidded down the streets to the boutique.

Our mountains weren't remote and glacial, like mountains on a calendar. They were shouldered together, round and close. Mostly they hovered, bent on worrying your mind. But this rare snow gentled them out a little.

I took in the freshness. "Ooh!"

We saw people we knew around Main. The convenience store was open; gas was flowing again. Colby put up his hand to wave. I puffed.

"Why the hell don't you have gloves on?"

"Because I always lose them," said Colby. "I've got work gloves. They stay at work."

"Lord, boy. You are a certain kind of idiot." We huddled together like skaters in a Currier & Ives print.

My father worked in antiques. He was as old as a grandpa and both his first and second wives were dead. The second one had been my sweet mother, and still I never thought of Dad as sinister – only wildly unlucky. I had two older half sisters; one was married with twin babies and the other one had a glamorous job. Neither of them had the time it took to look me up. Colby liked to announce that he was an only child.

We paused outside Ooh! La La. Despite the stupid cold, we blushed. You could get shy, living like we did. The owner had a metal bell boobytrapped in the door, this little bird struggling. Inside were a bunch of floor lamps, one with fringe, and an old green banker lamp next to the cash register. She sat on a piano stool, chilly as a mannequin, waiting. She had shiny-dark short hair and was dressed in a fuzzy white sweater and an unfashionably tight skirt, plus red boots made only for dancing. The first impression was a long Renaissance face, cut by freckles.

"Well, good morning," she said. "Lovely day, is it not?" She really meant it. Her voice was older than her face. I heard an old house with columns. Not the Queen Anne, but something a state or two further south.

She gave us each a business card with a man's name on it. *Stephens Smallwood, Proprietor.* I looked behind her. "It's me," she said. "Stephens is an old family name. People get used to it."

Colby started talking in his stricken way, and she pretended to appreciate his information. They were putting in a juice bar at the New Age Market, he told her. "I'm the front-end manager," he said.

I drifted away into Stephens' racks: mostly dresses from the '60s and '70s. Lots of polyester and purple-and-gold paisley. I fingered a slippery little sash. She was saying "mmm-hm, oh yes, mmm-hm" to Colby. But she was creeping up to me. She turned me around by the shoulders, and held me where she wanted me, and looked me up and down. "Narrow frame," she said. "But a large bosom. I bet bra shopping is not fun."

I forgot to ask her if I could sell my earrings in her store. I wiggled away from her, wiggled away from the cotton tank top inside my sweater. It was hard to remember the last time I'd worn a bra.

"I'm going to get a dressing room started for you," she said.

Colby and me, we gave each other a look. Where did she – where did *Stephens* – think she was doing business, exactly? *Get a dressing room started.* "Fine Consignments," the sign said.

If you wanted secondhand clothes around here, you went to Old Mission Thrift out on Laurel Cove Road, a barn hoarded up with treasures and a lot of moldy junk, where you could spend a whole hungover afternoon and not be bothered.

This was before the millennium turned over. The town hadn't been discovered yet by spiffy outsiders, the ones with new money and new ideas, a storm of them opening bistros and breweries and boutiques like this, curating the rents to oblivion. Stephens was a pioneer.

She had hung heavy tapestries from the ceiling, rigging them around exposed pipes and a couple of rods to form two dressing rooms. I punched the brocade. Already, I was stuck inside one of the enclaves, down to my tank top and underwear in front of an oval mirror with an ornate gold frame. I picked at it, knowing it was just painted plaster. "Piece of shit," I whispered.

She nudged a pair of limp brown boots under the curtain. "Vintage Frye," she said. "Made in the good old U. S. of A." I told her they were probably the wrong size. I was short, yes, so I appeared as though I might be small-footed, but it wasn't so.

There wasn't any mirror back at the house this long or clean, so I took a moment to look myself over. Large hanging breasts and a galaxy of moles, neck to thigh. The remnants of outraged teen skin pitting my face and chest. Still, though: a woman. Hair like a child raised by wolves was my pride.

The boots did fit, so I had to agree to buy them, and also this long slinky dress printed with something like cabbages. She pushed it on me, handed it over the top of the curtain almost seductively.

When I came out, Colby was wearing a cowboy shirt with pearl buttons and a rose on each pointy lapel. The guys in the band, they always wore shirts like that on stage, old-timey shirts, playing the traditional Appalachian ballads but giving them awkward new lyrics when it suited them. They redid the songs with a hyper twist, extending the jams to keep the crowds dancing – serious young guys swirling unsuspecting girls in the old-fashioned way, to get them dizzy.

I cleared my throat. "You'll sell a lot of those here," I told Stephens, nodding at Colby's shirt. "Retro chic." She clasped her hands like a praised child, and I had to look away. Colby fidgeted with the stiff cuffs of the shirt. He'd stopped wearing cowboy shirts once he realized the guys in the band were freezing him out. He'd gone back to his thermals and flannel.

"That was weird," I said. We were back in the cold, sliding around with our purchases wrapped in tissue paper and tucked neatly inside paper shopping bags with the Ooh! La La logo. "She'll never make it here. She's aristocratic or some shit."

"She's actually living in that building, though," said Colby. "I'm pretty sure one of those curtains had a bed behind it." He breathed ice. "I feel bad for her."

"Dude. Why would you feel bad for a girl with that kind of setup? She even smells like money."

"You just said she'll never make it in this shithole town."

"But if she does go down, she won't really struggle. She'll just take her inventory somewhere else."

"Ooh!" said Colby.

• • •

The world was too small. I gathered up his bag and mine and said goodbye to him at the New Age Market, went home and shoved through the front door, heavy with a brass knob, then up two flights to my turret. I put another log in the little woodstove next to my workbench, where I kept my pliers and clamps and beads and wire of five widths, all minuscule to untrained eyes.

I took off all my own clothes, put the flowered dress on, and lounged face up on my futon. I rubbed my belly in small circles. I wished Sunday was over, but beyond that, my blues were vague. I lifted one leg up in the air, lowered it, raised the other. Shapely calves, fleecy like a sheep. The dress was just sleazy polyester but it felt sensual, gliding down between my thighs.

I knew I had to get out. I could go to grad school and get a teaching degree, maybe Outdoor Education. I saw myself leading long hikes in the more remote sections of the Southern Appalachians, lecturing kids about the environment. I would be wise and reserved. Colby went camping with me, sometimes, when it was warmer and we could deal with the weather and one another's moods. When he was between girlfriends, I could count on him to be my partner in the woods.

I knew the difference between a poplar and an oak, even between a white oak and a red oak. A sycamore near the river was not the same as a runty sassafras. I could start good fires, I could purify water, and I knew where the best swimming holes were. Mostly I let Colby slack off and did all the work myself. He was a studious whittler.

Or maybe, instead, I would become a mother. Vader, one of the cats who belonged to the house, was on the futon beside me, curled up tight in a winter ball. There was enough of my long dress to share; I draped it over his body so we were in it together. I stroked his little cat back through the dress till I got a good purr going.

I had borrowed money from my father a few months ago, telling him it was for grad school application fees. But instead I went to the gynecologist, where they diagnosed scar tissue on my fallopian tubes. This was after my home cure had failed. I'd been brewing goldenseal tea, drinking quarts of it trying to fix what had to be some infection. I'd even peeled raw garlic and poked the bulbs deep inside me, wincing against the punishment. I hosted the intruders in there all night, easing them out in the morning like a thing forgiven. But none of it worked, and when I realized I'd been cradling the low ache through a whole season of changes in the tree colors on the ridge, I set about finding this doctor.

The scarring, it might mean I couldn't have children. Then again, if I saved up some money, I could have all of it scraped away. Plenty of women had this condition and went on to get pregnant, said the gynecologist. I asked her how I could figure out who had done this to me, and she smiled like I meant to be funny.

There weren't that many possibilities. But that didn't mean it would be easy to lay the blame. Kissing Vader on the bristly space between his closed eyes, I felt myself in danger of skating down the list again. I was headed into a terrific drowse.

• • •

Before I moved into the band house, I rented other rooms around town. I spent a few months with a carpenter who had his own cabin with a workshop attached; he got commissions to make enormous dining-room tables and was doing well for himself. He was older, divorced. I tried to remember the sex, but there had been so much late-night drinking that the details wouldn't come clear. I had a vision of him turning me over a lot, like a plank.

After him came a cook. He was from New Orleans and was sick of all the heat and sleaze there, so he said. He also said there was no place like New Orleans in the world, and definitely no culture in this backwards hole by comparison. He forgot to wash his hands after making me dinner one night, and later, when he tried to flower me open down there, his fingers flexed in the worst sort of peace sign, I screeched like a panther. It was the lingering habañero juice – my bad luck was unbelievable.

Who, then? Not many more options. I had loved this long-legged addict who loped into town one summer, boat in tow, eager for our clean, ancient rivers. He had medals – he'd made it to the Olympic trials for whitewater kayaking – but he had ruined his career by partying. The accident involved a tiki torch. He was too drunk to feel the pain – he must have been slow dancing with the torch. He must at least have addressed it face to face.

The thick pink skin grafts on his cheeks and neck and arms had nothing to do with his deeply tanned skin, the real bits of him left. The scarring dragged down his lower eyelids, so his eyes, although angry, seemed constantly pleading. His nose was melted down a little to meet his upper lip. The shock of that first meeting left you lightheaded.

He was still confident, though; his long river-rat hair had not been burned away. His sexiness was its own survivor. Even swallowing painkillers every hour, no chewing, this champion made the rounds.

He was arrogant. He should have apologized for his monstrous appearance, but that didn't happen. Once I had him alone, he rolled over me in waves, all that athletic discipline still alive and burrowing for an outlet. With light fingertips, I traced the bumpy trails on his back, where the fury on him wasn't so bad, wondering what maneuvers might be required to keep him to myself.

When he moved on to another town, I cried a lot and figured I was wounded now, too. It was then that I inched my way into the band house, moving in with my futon, my heirloom quilt from my dead mother's own childhood, my framed prints from Dad's collection – Maxfield Parrish, Winslow Homer – and two duffel bags of clothes. Plus my jewelry-making bench and chair. All of my tiny tools.

I never slept with any of the band guys, and I didn't count Colby; or rather, I didn't count the time I had found him in his room worrying over a redheaded college sophomore who'd had coffee with him twice before she slithered away, uncomfortable, to find a less earnest pursuer. I didn't intend to let him nurse a broken heart. I needed him to be strong. So I seduced him, scooting his pants down first, and then mine, and letting him go inside me for a few minutes until he thought better of it and we just hugged a while for comfort, a couple of ludicrous starfish.

That only left Boozer. His cackling laugh sickened me. His watery eyes worshipped me. He had two dogs, Rimbaud and Bukowski – big, smart, stinking mutts. They were rescue dogs, dead loyal but not reproachful. That was perfect liberty.

It's not like I wouldn't talk about it. I told the guys that whatever Boozer said in relation to me, sexually, was only his own drunken bullshit and perverted wishful thinking. The guitarist, who was also the lead singer, and the banjo player, the two of them mustered up a show of masculinity, an imitation of fathers. They nodded and squared their shoulders and promised to protect me.

But the fiddle player, a beautiful fool, he only laughed himself silly. Colby lectured him about what landlords were and were not allowed to do, according to the laws of our state.

When I woke up, the house was awake, too. I could hear instruments being taken up briefly and then forgotten. An appeal of minor-key strings. I heard voices. Most of the rooms had steam radiators that commenced to hissing and knocking as the winter afternoon darkened. The woodstove was mine alone. I got up, pulled on a pair of long johns, smoothed my dress down over them, poked at the fire, and sat down to work for a while.

Labyrinths were fashionable now, out of nowhere. A lot of people had started building labyrinths in their backyards, using rocks hauled up from the river, and my newest series of earrings was inspired by them. I entered a trance, making conical mazes out of wire. It took a while, shaping each cage around a Labradorite bead. I used my fingers until the possibilities ran out; then I took up my crimper. I would complete twenty pairs of the dangling labyrinths, I decided, and present them to Stephens to sell at Ooh! La La.

Because I was thinking about her, it wasn't as strange as it might have been when I realized her voice had joined the other voices downstairs. I got up and leaned over my staircase to make sure.

It was her. She was down there with Colby.

I stopped my work and shoved my feet into the Frye boots. I went down my attic stairs, then the main stairs, passed through the long hall and into the space we used as our living room – I guess it would have been called the parlor, once – and they were both there, sitting on the acid-yellow velvet couch, right up next to one another. The band guys were all hanging around, in the room and around the edges, trying to stir things up.

Stephens was looking appreciatively at the high ceilings, the broken medallion chandelier, the tall windows, the faded toile wallpaper showing children struggling to enjoy themselves on giant Victorian bicycles. She had a bottle of wine nestled between her and Colby, and they were drinking from coffee mugs. Their eyes glittered.

"Must have been a short shift," I said to Colby. He reminded me it was Sunday, when the New Age Market closed early.

"This is quite the abode you have here," said Stephens. "I wouldn't be at all surprised if you told me you had ghosts."

"Darlene is our ghost," said the lead singer/guitarist, throwing his head in my direction – he was the gentleman of the bunch. He was leaning against the mantelpiece, lashes half lowered, studying a spot around Stephens' knees, which were smooth and bare and substantial, greeting everyone under that tight pencil skirt.

The grand fireplace in the room was so neglected it was considered a fire hazard, so we had filled the charred gap with a bunch of different-sized candles instead. Most of the time no one bothered to light them, but right now every one of them was ablaze.

"Actually," I said, sinking gradually to the floor, "if you feel weird energy, it's because this was a home for teenage mothers at one point, in the '50s I think. Or early '60s." The unwed mothers' babies would be older than us now, I had figured out once, but still younger than our parents.

"They adopted all the babies out," I said, looking at her. "The mothers weren't even allowed to see them after they were born."

Stephens pouted.

"Well, we don't know for sure if it's true," said Colby. "But our landlord said something about it."

"Public record," I said.

The banjo player was worrying his floppy hair with his fingers and talking about the band's upcoming tour. Killing Frost was playing fifteen shows in the lowland states in January and February. They were on a label now. The deal was so close to being done – they were going to get paid for most of these dates. The fiddler nodded from his usual place in the living room's only rocking chair, his legs spread apart and his fists poised like gargoyles on top of his thighs. "It's all happening," he said.

"We go into the studio in March to make our first CD," said the lead singer/guitarist. He wasn't one to get excited.

I blushed a little for Colby. Colby wanted to be a producer. Either that or a promoter. He wouldn't turn out to be either one, though – he wasn't blessed with any talent except the most ghastly sincerity. This studio, it was two hundred miles away, set up in an old church full of stained glass. All the best alt-country bands made their records there, if they could. Killing Frost wouldn't be needing Colby and his little pieces of recording equipment anymore.

"Too bad we're setting out before you have a chance to hear us," the banjo player said to Stephens. "We'll probably fit in a local gig in the spring, though. Homecoming show."

"Watch Boozer raise the fucking rent while we're gone," said the fiddler, bucking against the rocker. "Our landlord is a psycho."

"Boozer will have to find new renters soon, anyway," said the lead singer/guitarist. He wasn't as handsome as the fiddler, but he was aware of his appeal. He wouldn't swear the first time he met a lady, and he liked to use phrases from old movies. "We're not long for this flophouse," he drawled.

Colby said Stephens should definitely check out Killing Frost the next time she had a chance. Just then he was a fool for amnesty. "We're all going to be able to say we knew them when," he said.

I watched him attempt to be everywhere, his loyalty on fire. But in the next breath, he excused Stephens from the pressures of fandom. "She's insanely busy getting her shop running," said Colby. "Entrepreneur life."

They were both in retail, I realized. The New Age Market and Ooh! La La were only separated by a steep alley.

"Having my grand opening after a blizzard," said Stephens. "Not smart." She pantomimed suicide, a little pearl-handled revolver to the head. "I got ahead of myself. But I love snow."

I whispered "Ooh!" to the chandelier.

Now she was backtracking to music. She mentioned her dead grandfather, who'd had a fiddle he kept locked up. It was from the 1880s, and if you touched it, you'd get a whipping with a willow branch. It was her Nana who did the threatening.

"He called it a fiddle," said Stephens. "But Nana always referred to it as 'the violin.' It was their point of contention."

"He must have played songs for her, though," said Colby. "People expressed themselves differently then. He wouldn't have said 'I love you.'"

"Speak of the devil," said the lead singer/guitarist, "and in he walks." He was late on his cue, though, because no one had said Boozer's name for at least fifteen minutes. There he was, though, stomping in through the back door in a snow-covered Carhartt jacket and a squashed-down fedora. He stroked melting flakes out of his greasy beard. The dogs followed.

Stephens introduced herself. "It's a family name," she said. Boozer bowed and introduced the dogs. "Rimbaud here," he said, pointing one way. "Bukowski there." I was still sitting on the floor near Colby, my chin on my knees, staring over my boots at the flickering candles, my new dress strewn around me like an oil spill. Bukowski flopped down beside me, panting. He was part cattle dog; he had the longer coat.

Boozer looked around his living room like any satisfied patriarch. "You've made friends with the illustrious Colby, yes?" He rolled his own cigarettes and always kept one tucked in the brim of the fedora. I saw him fumble around for it with his thick, dirty hand. "How do you like mountain life so far?"

"I'm so happy to be here," said Stephens, "I can hardly even tell you." She did her smile and smoothed her smooth hair. Then she took a long, draining sip, stretched rudely past Colby, and chunked me on the top of my shoulder bone with her empty mug. "Behold this goddess right here," she said. "Tell me what y'all think of the dress and boots yours truly picked out for her."

I moved my head in a slow circle to regard her. The flowery outbursts – was it her own way, or a parody of something, like maternal violence? This wasn't a rhythm I would try to enter. But there we all were, letting her get away with it.

"Looking good there, Darlene," said the banjo player, heading to the kitchen for more beer.

"Darlene is the most down-to-earth artist you will ever meet," said Colby.

"Are you an artist?" Stephens said, widening her eyes. She reminded me of a silent-film star, but I would never remember the actress' name. She set her mug against her naked knees. "What do you do? You seem like a deep person, so I'm getting ready to be wowed by your work."

I didn't answer. Colby would talk about my earrings for me. I was busy curling Bukowski's thick dog lips up high over his fangs and gently letting them drop. He always let me do this. I dug my hand into his long, smelly coat; if I went in at a slant, my fingers would disappear up to the knuckle.

But Stephens interrupted Colby. "I want to call her Janis," she said. "To me Darlene looks just like Janis Joplin. The wild frizzy hair." She laughed beautifully. "And her face, too. Homely-pretty. She just needs the little round glasses."

Colby said, "Hey, now – what?" But that was all. The heat of my face and the heat of the candles came together so well I was nearly sick. I was standing up in slow motion, so I could run away, but the fiddler wouldn't respect the silence.

His tastes weren't as snooty as the other guys in the band would have liked them to be; he didn't get into antique 78s or historic tablature. He was a bit of an embarrassment, despite his popularity. He still had posters in his room, like any kid. "Janis died at age twenty-seven," he said. "Like Kurt Cobain. The 27 Club."

Colby helped him. "And Jimi Hendrix," he said. "And Jim Morrison."

Boozer waited a discreet interval before he followed me back up to my room. I had taken off the dress – ripped it off – and was lying on my futon in my tank top and long underwear, belly down, my face resting against my forearms. Too limp to kick off my boots. His smell haunted the stairs several steps ahead of him. He was quiet for a minute, pausing for my mood. Then he walked over and sat on the edge of the old mattress, making it dip. His bad knee popped.

"Heyyyyy, Janis," he said. His loud shadow disturbed Vader, who woke up, groomed a paw, and turned his head to the wall.

Boozer tried to wait out my silence. But he couldn't manage everything.

"What did that girl with the guy's name say you were? Pretty homely?" He patted my back. "Come on, now."

I was sniffing my arm, up and down. Keeping my scent to myself. "You're too smart to let that snotty bitch get you down," Boozer said. "Who the fuck sent her, anyway?"

"Where are the dogs?" I said, "I don't want you up here. I'm going to call them."

"Don't be like that," said Boozer. He flicked at my hip, then used the same hand to massage his knee. "Be glad. Good riddance to your shadow, right? Now Colby can follow her around for a change. You've got better things to do with your time. And I brought you some free firewood, girl, so cheer up."

He had dumped it on the floor. Out there in what was now night, the locust branch hit my round antique window, shaking snow loose like a lace handkerchief.

I could get up. I could. I would. I would busy myself, talk about poetry with Boozer. The Romantics, the Beats. He was fun to talk to, sometimes. He had more education than any of them, was the irony. I could warm up a tool in the fire. My best bent-nose pliers. I could put the long flowered dress back on, hide the pliers in all the folds, get old Boozer in a slow hug and then catch him by surprise, stab him in the nuts or in his too-wide ass with what I had crafted: a flaming spear. Smush a boot toe in his face after he went down. I could throw all my duffel bags in the fire and go down to Ooh! La La and buy a round hatbox suitcase, the old-timey kind, and one outfit, a dress of my own choosing. A short one. I'd show off my legs, cold as it was, dig out the Escort, and leave forever. It wasn't ever as hard as I made it out to be.

But right now I was still laying belly down. "Go ahead and rent my room to Stephens," I said. I felt my lips vibrate against my arm. If I went blind and deaf, I could always communicate this way with myself. "Rent my room to Stephens."

"What now?"

I raised my head. "I said, rent my room to Stephens. Colby seems to think she needs a place to stay, because Colby now has no balls as well as no brains. This is my last week here."

"Aw, Christ," said Boozer. "Take it easy. You've just got cabin fever. You ought to be used to that by now. You're a mountain girl, not some flatlander."

Now I was on my elbow. "Here's what I want to say," I said. I guess I had been wanting to say it for a while. "Fuck you, Boozer. Fuck you, fuck everyone, and fuck all of this. But you most of all. Do you hear me? I said fuck you and the mother that made you."

I got up, kicked past him, crossed the room in a leap, and made a sweep of my tools for emphasis, dragging my arm across my worktable, scattering the pliers and clamps and metal and beads and semi-precious gems up in the air, this little glittering storm, trusting at least half of them to fall back down unbroken.

Antique Power Association

All this was a while ago, the stone age, before we developed more than one or two ways to feel hurt forever. It sort of began around bread.

The Trappist monks at Genevieve Abbey, they still bake this whole-grain organic bread they call Holy Loaves. In those days, we didn't know it was organic or even what organic was – but then again, the monks were always ahead of everyone else. They packaged it themselves, merrily, seemingly without complaint, and sold it for a benevolent sum to the public: in local groceries, and, after a while, in health-food stores and fancy bakery-slash-cafés, when that scene preened into life.

Today, I see, they've developed a real brand, even selling hoodies and bumper stickers from their website. All their prices got higher.

The abbey itself – made inside and out of river rock – it just gets older and older. The monks never built a new one, just made repairs here and there, a new roof, a magic trick of solar panels, and registered the building with the Historical Society people. It was sited in the mid-1800s beneath a tower of unsheared firs, but it's not the oldest building in our rural village, which sits in a hard valley high north on I-81. Not even the oldest building by far.

Genevieve Abbey opened itself to visitors decades ago. The monks invited normal people into their sanctuary to appreciate their noble values. Oh, it was all about the rustic life and the wonderful hard work.

During this era, before the monks knew the possibilities of the treasure they harbored, churning out all that organic bread, all that craft beer, the smallest of my many cousins, a four-foot eleven part-time ski instructor, began spending lots of time at the abbey. She claimed to love God – all the plaques in her house said so – and she made friends among the monks: volunteering for them, repeating their cause, gaining comfort from their everyday rituals (this I could picture very well).

At home, though, she had lost her faith. Sheela had borne three children with her husband, a bucket-jawed provider who stood six-foot four. When his favorite team was losing, it didn't matter what sport, but it was probably football, Mitch would lose his dignity all over their TV screen. I won't tell you what he yelled; it insults decent people – but almost everything else about him signified a traditional family man.

Sheela wasn't happy, though, and her complaint was specific. Slowly, she began to come out with it, choosing unlikely places for her confession. She was hushed, blushing, but it was all wrong. She began her mission in the summer, that short precious time! We barely got three months.

"He's too big for me." She whispered it to her friends, to her brothers and sisters, to all of us cousins, even to strangers, creeping bucket in hand, row to row, through the rows of blueberry bushes, acres of them, at our uncle's U-pick farm, where she worked every season for pocket money – where we all put in time.

If some of us first assumed she meant the drastic difference in their heights, we were enlightened by her next sentence: "He doesn't care that it hurts me."

This intimate reference wasn't shocking, really, only a puzzle. Sheela wasn't a newlywed; she was a PTO leader. She had married young. Her youngest child was in kindergarten and her oldest was already a teenager. It failed as a revelation. This wasn't urgent; it was only embarrassing.

Our land is fertile when it wants to be, only carved by harsh seasons. Even after we elected Reagan and let him bleed out our farms, some stores in the area – all these little markets – kept their wooden floors.

We meet emergency with practicality here. I'm saying we still do. Snowfalls can be so heavy they implode windows, but it's just dealt with. Violence is antique. Even today, after our recovery, our advances, young men's fingers are lost to hay balers. Patriarchs are devoured by combines.

Left without sympathy, Sheela turned to the monks, to that refuge of celibacy where she could chat about Christ's love and fill her small, sore body with the dark ale and the chanting, the scripture and the root vegetables, the bread, and, in season, the rosemary-sprinkled Christmas cake. (It was a treat said to invite communion with a higher realm, where more important things were happening than what was troubling her down here.)

But one unloving afternoon full of Allegheny ice, Sheela drank a heavy, home-brewed monk's beer, and then another and another. She curled off her Shaker sweater and curled down her drawstring jeans – I conjured this detail; it wasn't hard to see – and slipped out of everything underneath, and approached a young seminarian in his bare, drafty room.

"I mean, what a friggin slut, right?"

That was one of Sheela's younger brothers, Lance, a college student in the city and the cousin closest to my age. He was home on his Christmas break when it all happened. Lance and I were born only a few months apart and had a special bond, even though I wasn't a guy. I was just an only child and a high-school graduate, but I hadn't left home yet. I took classes at the community college and looked after my sick folks. Mama and Daddy were going to go early, were already well on their way, from all the heavy smoking.

I lit a cigarette myself and let Lance snort a minute about the situation.

"Keep going, man," I said. I kicked him. "I want to know everything." (Armed only with a two-year degree, I eventually found my living running a little newspaper based out of the next town over, which had a good three thousand more people living in it than our town did. Landing this job, it was really a miracle, the kind of small-town foolishness that could never happen now. I sent photographers to shoot stories about barbecue fundraisers – usually held for the families of accident victims – and assigned reporters to cover important local deaths. Mama and Daddy bragged about me so much I knew I'd hit the right path. I developed an editor's tone, brisk but guarded, always longing a little after poetry. I found I was made for this work.)

"I need to know exactly what she did." I was trying to be serious. This was before anyone in the world got troubled with the idea of personal boundaries. This thing had happened, and it wouldn't unhappen if we didn't talk about it. I'm sure we were all wrong, but we weren't unhappy about it.

We were sitting next to one another on crappy red bar stools, snug inside our Main Street's one place for this kind of camaraderie, a bar called Cheap Chuck's. The Friday-night fish fry was all over but the breeze of grease, and the rowdier pool crowd was starting to fill in the gaps. Drifts from the most recent storm had been shoveled away from the entrance, but one crescent-shaped wedge of snow was still stuck to the bar's front door, like a wave stranded incredibly far from the beach.

"All right," he said. "All right. So she has a hard-on for this one guy, right? He's training to be a monk. Really young. Fat."

"He was fat?"

"Hell! I don't know. He was big. Tall. Sheela likes big guys." We pictured Mitch, big all over.

"How could they be fat eating homemade bread all day?" I said.

"That's how you get fat," Lance informed me.

"What was his name?" I said.

"I didn't ask," he said. "Why the hell would I ask? So she's got him in her sights, right? Volunteering over there and whatnot. Flirting. Praying with him and shit like that. She's not looking to leave Mitch, she just wants an affair, someone to pay attention to her."

"She wants a smaller guy. Down there," I reminded him.

"She must have figured, this idiot actually wants to be a monk and he's not even old, he's got to be the exact opposite of a stud," Lance agreed.

"So was he?"

"She never gets far enough to find out. She never even kisses him, she tells me. She has all her clothes off, just ready to go, you know, and this fucking dimwit, he starts to cry."

"Holy … holy," I said. "What was wrong with him?"

"He started to cry. He was intimidated," said Lance, with a hard suck on his beer like I didn't know jack crap.

"Well, then, what was wrong with her?"

"What's wrong with her? Sheela does whatever the hell Sheela wants, that's what's wrong with her," he said. "She's always been that way. Remember when Gramps used to give us rides on the Farmall? We were just little rugrats."

"Naturally."

"All right, well. She got mad as shit one time because we'd been taking turns and she thought she was getting shorter rides than me. I don't know why she thought that. Because she was a girl, I guess. The corn was up, that much I do recall. So it was summer. Gramps puts her down and starts to pull me up, and Sheela realizes her ride's over again and goes running and crying back to the house to bitch to Gram about it. You can see her mouth open catching flies, even though the Farmall's so loud out in that field you can't really hear her. Goddamn screaming to wake the dead, though, you can tell that without the sound down."

I laughed big time, my mouth falling open in an imitation of the scream.

"Right! Mad as hell because she can't have ten more seconds on the goddamn tractor. So me and Gramps, we're starting our ride out there, and all of a sudden Sheela stops dead and turns around mid-run. Picture it, it's like a basketball game – it's like she's got the ball but she's gone crazy and now she's going to make a basket for the other team. Right? So instead of going to the house, she starts running toward that little side field where they used to keep that old pony."

"Dink! The little mare."

"Uh-huh, yup. Broken-down Dink with an electric fence." Now Lance was laughing, too. "Kept her from running away to the glue factory, maybe. But the fence is on, and Sheela either knows this or not, but we figure later she must have known it was on because of all of the times they used to warn us about it, remember? And then this happens – get this – she's so pissed she goes up and grabs the goddamn fence, both hands on it like this. Completely on purpose. I don't know how much electricity went through her, but it would have killed someone smarter than her. Hell. But she's just hanging on like the devil's bitch, and she can't let go till Gramps knocks off the juice at the source. Either that or she won't let go."

"I do remember. I remember everyone talking about it." And I did. I remembered the long aftermath, these hot waves of elated gossip, but not the day itself. Now I imagined an infuriated little Sheela, her hair flaming out behind her like a horse's mane, not old Dink but a unicorn or at least a palomino – the scene frozen and inspiring, like a calendar photo. Had it happened like that?

"Sheela will do anything," I said, and ordered a St. Pauli Girl. We still had the Christmas spirit, and I felt like treating myself.

"She's a friggin nut and definitely a bit of a whore," said Lance. I'd never seen anyone look so proud.

What Sheela was offering to the monk was clear, but what she was hoping to get back, the exact nature of it, is still a mystery to me. After he declined her challenge, the poor novitiate, and after she was reported, a meeting took place. Gently and unforgivingly, the lot of them banned her from the abbey for life.

After that, events ran a more natural course. Sheela arranged for a trial separation from her husband and found a banker lover, a bland older man. He fell hard for her earthy, low-ebb charms; you wouldn't expect anything different. He couldn't tell a story, our family's trait, I guess. Our test. And so, although he treated her well, he was barely tolerated.

Her mother and father were especially disapproving. So grumpy, so pissed. They seethed and seethed. Pious to the last atom, they didn't consider divorce an option for their only daughter.

Sheela had gotten hammered and stripped nude in front of a man wed to God. Everyone knew about it, but the reaction never grew past a shrug. In such a ruthless landscape, these things happened. No one in the family stopped buying Holy Loaves.

But on another day, a little later that year, Sheela, not yet legally free, appeared at her oldest son's wrestling match holding hands with her mild-mannered new boyfriend. Her offended parents, who never missed a grandchild's game or play or recital, got up from their front-row bleacher seats without speaking and walked out of the gym. Stalked.

In our close town, sprung and bound by the ties of kin, they sinned deeply. I don't mean Sheela and her boyfriend. I mean her mother and father. Attempting to fuck a monk: that was bad. Appearing at school with your lover when your divorce wasn't yet final – that was worse still.

In our eyes, though, the way the rest of us saw it, neither of Sheela's crimes compared to what her parents did. Leaving a grandchild's high-school sporting event meant deserting the alma mater that had educated the family since the days of inkwells in the wooden desks; since dire willow-branch beatings in the basement.

They were ditching their own blood! So I'm saying, poking around for solace at Genevieve Abbey, whatever Sheela did, or had tried to do, how could that be immoral? Winter was winter was winter.

My own mother was the sister of Lance and Sheela's mother, but by this time, Mama was far too faded to enjoy the scandal. At the expected time, and in her own sweet, unadorned way, she died. Daddy went next, and after I buried them and finished up my grieving, I began to care more about the future. I quit smoking and found my own lover, a volleyball coach. We had the same first name – another miracle – although I went by Jenny, still, and she was called Jen. For a little while, Lance was the only cousin who would speak to me honestly about her: about my friend, as the rest of the family carefully called her. About my love.

I kept on with my job and fiddled with headline after headline, romancing my puns: *Hayne County's Antique Power Association Accelerates Community Involvement, Holds Vintage Tractor Show ... Lady Yellow Jackets Buzz Ahead to State Finals.*

Meanwhile, it was cold. Again. What seemed like half the year, the wind blasted over us from the glacial fields to our north, echoing the wasted fury of the last Ice Age.

Acknowledgments

Three stories in this collection were previously published in print literary magazines: "The Ballad of Cherrystoke" appeared in the 2020 Summer Prize Issue of *Mississippi Review*. "It's Called Overwintering" appeared in the 2020-21 Fall/Winter edition of *The Chattahoochee Review*. "Antique Power Association" appeared under the title "The Wasted Fury" in the Winter 2018-19 edition of *Moth Magazine*.

The song Dinah and Shad sing in "Ballad of Cherrystoke" is Child Ballad 243 – a Scottish-derived ballad known by various titles including "The House Carpenter," "The Daemon Lover," and "James Harris" – as interpreted in versions collected from Madison County, North Carolina.